EAGLES OVER BIG SUR

"It was always a wild rocky coast, desolate and forbidding to the men of the pavements, eloquent and enchanting to the Taliessins. The homesteader never failed to unearth fresh sorrows."

—HENRY MILLER
Big Sur and the Oranges of Heironymous Bosch

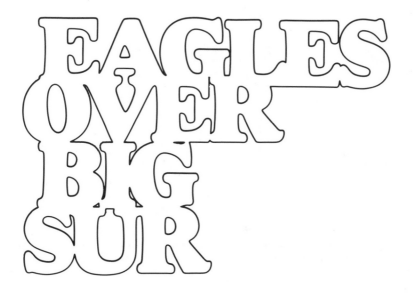

Jack Curtis

A *Noel Young Book*

CAPRA PRESS
Santa Barbara/1981

*For Micah, Lincoln, Melissa Jane and Ross,
my children, my compadres.*

ACKNOWLEDGEMENTS

Another version of "Lion in the Rain-Rinsed
Morning" appeared in the *Atlantic Monthly*
and *Reader's Digest*, a variant of "The Gentle
Shepherd" was published by *Sports Illustrated*.

Cover design by Peggy Brogan.
Typography by Terri Wright.

Library of Congress Cataloging in Publication Data

Curtis, Jack.
    Eagles over Big Sur.

    I. Title.
PS3505.U866E18   813'.54   80-25855
ISBN 0-88496-160-5

EAGLES OVER BIG SUR

*In Big Sur, forty years ago, Apple Pie Inn was crushed
under earth sliding off an unnamed ridge which leaped steeply
on up to a beautiful and brutal heaven, and when Harry and
Greta pioneered their family homestead up there, they named
it Apple Pie Ranch . . .*

1.

Any Natural Place

THREE DAYS BEFORE the Fourth of July party, Harry McAlister stood outside in the dawn welcoming the sun and the early morning birds and watching a little scar of moon fade into the western sea.

From the back porch, the sky to the east looked like bubbling champagne, a billion billion golden electrons swirling and blaring and bouncing around in a wild retort behind Pico Blanco.

And he thought that any natural place, whether desert, or tundra, or the Ventana Wilderness next door, contained a special fear, and yet after mastering a multitude of tiny harmonies, a man discovered his most sublime moments in the magnitude of slow turning stars, the minute miracle of a hummingbird's egg, or as now, in the suffusion of fresh light coming over the black scarps and ridges that ended the continent.

While the pale light boiled pink and golden behind the silhouetted summit, northward in shadow the brassy slopes of wild oat pastures stepped down to the ocean, and far to the west stood raddle-headed Point Sur, a monumental seastack

7

topped by a stone lighthouse and nearly surrounded now by the surf of high tide mopping around its base, and on beyond from his elevation, he could see clear to the dark curve of the world, a peacock-blue convex world daubed with a couple tiny fishing boats.

"Come to the party, fishermen!" he called. "Bring a fish!"

Silly old man, he thought, if you lived in town they'd lock you up.

And for a fine moment he thought of three tall sons in Australia. Strong men he had helped plan and start and who came through on their own. Their remembrance was a part of the strength and beauty of the morning, great broad-chested Vikings, taking their physiques and coloring from his wife's side, stepping out of the swimming pool below the garden, water dripping from their auburn beards, strong in sex, their teeth white when they smiled. They'd be back, but not a chance of them making the Fourth.

Even when he turned his eyes southward toward Rupture Ridge, it didn't look all that bad. The long feminine profile of the rise lay graceful as a sleeping nude, shadows covering the blotches of buildings and bulldozed pads. Once it had been too steep, too shaded, too isolated for housing, and the land so poor it couldn't be grazed or farmed. The old timers had thought Mr. Jennings was demented when he carved up the cliff into five acre lots and called them ranchettes. Jennings was first.

He resolved not to lose the good sweetness of the morning with sour thoughts of developments and zoning and he kept his eyes going on around to the east where the sun came marching up like a goddamned brass band over Pico Blanco, and he nearly laughed himself silly again.

But catching himself, he muttered to the distant mountain, "We're sun's people, free borne eagles, writing on the stones and fields with our shadows; making, leaving no marks other than ourselves, and no wound save maybe a tone of feathered air."

He picked a few chard leaves from the garden and took a

shortcut to the horse pasture where Billy, the bay Morgan colt, stood waiting with his ears pointing, his skin like polished walnut, and Harry laid his face against the colt's warm neck.

He'd kept a Jersey cow when the kids were young, and he had felt the same rapport with her when he nestled his face in her moist, warm flank and hot milk misted from the bucket between his knees.

He went to the barn to feed the cats. Like everything else, he'd picked a special breed of cat for its special function. These were Manx, fire crackers, top guns, pest controllers deluxe.

The black Manxs purred around his legs. Lemon eyes, short-haired, high-haunched, savage cats, ancient Egypt in their poise. Masters of their places.

The barn, which had gradually become half warehouse, was jammed with spare appliances and tires and mattresses and household goods of his daughters and sons. Separate bins held a variety of builder's supplies, because the nearest hardware store was thirty miles away. And the tanning gear, the apple press, the beekeeping equipment, the ropes and cables and chains, broadaxes, adzes, peavies, wedges, draw knives, so much varied stuff in that two-story barn he supposed maybe it was worth a small fortune.

He kept the woodshop separate and inviolable. A desk built of curly redwood burl slabs stood almost finished. He hadn't made the desk in a hurry and if it survived fire, flood, and the H-bomb, it would last a couple thousand years at least. Why push on the hours?

He ran his hand along the polished top. It was like touching Billy's soft and responsive neck.

Closing the door of the sweet-smelling shop, he walked on to the chicken house, a structure he'd built for pure carpentry pleasure, every detail in it fine as Chippendale.

Like horse, cat or his black retriever, the breed of poultry was determined by its rightness here on the ridge. Softly colored golden birds with strong characters, the Buff Or-pingtons were just broody enough to keep the flock young each year, hatching out chicks to replace themselves and put some tasty roosters on the table too.

"Talk, talk, talk," he answered the hens in their own peculiar falsetto, and proceeded on to the sheep pasture.

He had selected Cheviots for their handsomeness and durability. Their clean white faces carried intelligent brows and delicate features, their wool was deep and fitted neatly over their shoulders like a Tudor cape, and they were stubborn individuals of Scottish origin much like Harry himself. In these hills they foraged on the brush, removing fuel from hillsides that could burn like gasoline in the summer. Five ewes, Mac, the ram, and seven roly-poly white lambs.

He poured a bucket of cracked corn into their trough and let them snuffle and grind it down. Like the chickens, he'd experimented with other breeds—Suffolks, Hampshires, Dorsets—but they were of a lowland character and wouldn't fight, didn't thrive on the hard go. These sheep mated his spirit, and in that sunbeam moment, he realized that everything on the whole ranch had come to be a selection that matched his own sense of tenacity and faith in the ridge life. The vegetables he grew came from seed he kept, even the orchard was a mirror of himself. And he suddenly saw himself as a composite of Washington navels, Nabal avocados, sweet Apple Pie Ridge tomatoes, Manxs, Labs, Morgans, Buffs, Cheviots. All Harry McAlister!

Back at the house, he washed his hands and went into the big-windowed dining room brilliant with sunshine. The Van Wingerden paintings on the walls burned with color, and the smell of cooking ham and eggs came from the kitchen.

"Hey, Beauty," he yelled. "What's for breakfast?"

"Beer and oysters," Greta called back.

"I can't wait!" He went into the kitchen and affectionately touched her hip.

Her hair was the kind of soft red that never grays. To him she still looked like a Norwegian travel poster, rosy cheeks, freckles, cornflower blue eyes, and she aged without showing it except for a few sun wrinkles and a stiff ankle from an old fracture.

"Harry," she said as they sat at the big table cluttered with papers and drawing materials and vegetable seeds, such a generous table that one end could hardly care what happened on the other, "Harry—maybe we should skip the Fourth of July."

"Sure. It's only my birthday," he said with easy sarcasm.

"I mean skip the usual big bash."

"Heck, I thought we might make it bigger. Get the community tied together instead of tearing apart."

"It's too late," she said, "Bickering, back-biting, anonymous letters, now one group is talking about incorporating."

"Why not show them how the old coasters had a good time and worked out their problems on the side?" He searched his lean, work-warped fingers for berry stickers.

"Harry," she shook her head and smiled, "you're a dreamer."

"How else they going to know the good life? We get those pushy city folks up here to see the practical side, see how to really live with the land instead of building cliff houses out of sheetrock, they'll start working harder and cut out all this push for power."

"Harry—"

"I have to kill the crippled lamb anyway," he said.

"You want me to send out invitations?"

"Oh hell no. Just pass the word around that everyone's welcome."

"There'll be a mob."

He felt good just thinking about people playing volleyball in the pasture, ping pong, and horseshoes, and dancing on the deck, and strolling around through the flowers and looking at how the ranch functioned.

"I'll make a batch of moonshine and get a keg of beer."

"Crazy dreamer."

"Wait'll you see all the people swimming and playing games and dancing in the moonlight!" He tried to ease her doubts.

About noon a little yellow Volkswagen came in the driveway and out popped Penny, her loose black hair twisting like a shimmering shawl almost to her waist, her blue eyes shining.

She gave Harry a big hug before he had assimilated the simple fact that she'd come home again.

She'd managed it at least once a year since she was thirteen. Thank heaven her sister, little Julia, had married an engineer and moved to Saudi Arabia.

"Hiya, Pops." Penny kissed his eroded cheek, hugged him again, and spoke through the open window. "Come on, Moe, say hello to your grandpops."

Harry opened the passenger door and hoisted the little black lad into his arms and squeezed him hard.

"Hello, Mohammed," he said, putting the boy down, stooping to look into the dark eyes and tousling his harum-scarum afro. "I'm glad you've come up to help."

Moe's worried eyes darted about.

"Say 'hello', Moe!" Penny's tone was shrill.

"Easy now. We're goin' to farm, aren't we, Moe?"

The boy barely nodded, still not speaking.

"And maybe later on we'll shoot the rifle at a bottle."

Moe stared, disbelieving. "Really?"

"Sure, and we're goin' to have a party. Goin' to be a lot of people up here."

Again the eyes darted about.

"Probably a bunch of kids your age will come and you'll have some friends to play with."

"Can I sleep with the horse?" Moe asked, dark fawn eyes round and wonderful.

"I don't know why not, Moe."

"Well, I do," Penny said.

"I guess you can throw sticks for Poky." Harry tried to take the bite out of her denial.

"You're just in time for coffee," Greta greeted them from the front porch. "And there's a cupcake for a good boy, too."

Maybe it'll work this time, Harry said a little prayer in his head; following them all through the kitchen and out on the western deck.

He sat with them, not saying anything, nor listening much either.

"...late to work...the old man wanted a little more than the rent..."

"Sure, Penny, just take your old room and pitch in."

He noticed tiny lines around her eyes, and a bruise almost hidden by her hair. At twenty-three her figure was turning slack.

It hurt to see the obvious, like a green apple blown off the tree, a lamb born twisted.

Maybe she's over it, maybe she'll turn around...go to school...find a home...find a career...find herself...

"I can use a little break."

Her fingernails were long as silver spoons.

"I'm goin' to hike around the west pasture," Harry yawned.

"Go on, Moe, wear yourself out," Penny said.

Moe took Harry's hard bent hand.

"We're going to see if the sheep have eaten all the grass on the knoll," Harry said.

They strolled down the sidehill lane, redwinged blackbirds singing, phoebes darting off the brush tops for flying bugs, and a pair of redtails hawking in long high circles their steep dominion, and on west sugar-white surf kept curling in.

When they reached the meadow on the point, Harry heard Mac's bell and saw the flock feeding below him.

Moe counted them off, and in the counting noticed the crippled lamb.

"What will happen to him?"

"Moe, he'll be killed first, but sooner or later all of these animals will be slaughtered."

"When will you do it?"

"Tomorrow. You'll learn the meaning of meat."

"I don't think I want to watch."

Harry sat on the grass and watched the sheep graze over milky wild oats. He pulled a stalk and chewed on it. Moe pulled a stalk and chewed. The golden sun brought in a life of its own, pumping strong juices into Harry's old bones.

"How old are you now, Moe?"

"Seven. I'll be in second grade."

"Like school?"

"Can we go look at the horse?"

"You're a busy guy. Why don't you lie back and watch that big sheep cloud eat the sky and listen to the birds and grasshoppers?"

"I might go to sleep."

"Heck, I take a nap out here every once in awhile. I remember one time back in Kansas when I was about your age, I lay down in the cornfield in the first spring sunshine, and it felt so good I went to sleep and everybody thought I was a strange one."

"I'm a strange one too," Moe said from his dream.

"That's the best kind," Harry murmured, drifting off into the eye of the suffusing sun.

On the morning of July second at the sheep pen, Harry released all but the cripple. The flock of knobby-browed elders stood and looked at him with set, blue-gray eyes, nostrils pulsing, white heads and cockle shell ears up and attentive. The lonely one in the pen limped along the fence and blatted, while the flock pretended to graze, sniffing the ground, covertly watching. Harry thought they knew more about the knife and the shepherd than he.

Guardians of my soul,
Christ, grant this lamb
Green grass
In the land of the dead.

Harry quietly turned and scuffled his fingers through Moe's kinky hair.

They walked to the pen where the wether waited patiently now, his future already known.

Harry took the pistol from his back pocket and looked into those gray eyes that were seeing from the desert of Judea when gods walked behind their flocks. He placed the muzzle of the pistol against the clean white forehead and fired. Knees buckled and head dropped. The lamb slumped, properly killed.

Quickly Harry opened the gate, grabbed both kicking hind-legs and dragged the lamb downhill a hundred feet to an overhanging oak.

"I must cut his throat now, so the meat will be bled properly," Harry said, and drove the sticking knife into the throat just behind the wether's ear. Bright arterial blood gushed hot and foaming over his hand.

With a curved skinning knife he flayed the breast, then shoved the wooden gambrel into cuts between tendon and ankle, hooked onto block and tackle, and pulled the carcass clear of the ground.

After he'd fisted off the hide, Harry took a small knife and pierced the upper abdomen. Guiding the point of the blade with two fingers on his left hand, he brought the cut down to the brisket without piercing the paunch. Gray entrails pushed against the back of his hand, but he held the cascade of still-pulsing guts until the cut was complete. The scent of the basic animal came out with them.

Harry pointed out each organ to the boy, intestines, spleen, liver, kidneys, heart, lungs.

"Grampa," Moe asked after awhile, "do black people have black guts?"

"No, everybody's got the same color guts," Harry laughed. "No difference at all."

He cut off the front feet, cross-hatched a witch design on each thigh, put a clean cloth on his shoulder and carried the carcass inside to hang and cool.

"That's it, Moe. The wether was born right over there in the little pasture, he grew fat on the grass we watered, and nothing is wasted. He feeds us and the ground, same as he was fed."

"I guess it's all right." Moe looked off at the hills.

They went into the house and scrubbed the blood and fat from their hands.

Penny came into the kitchen, still in her night robe, combing her hair.

"Early birders," she grumbled. "Don't you ever sleep?"

"Hell's afire, Penny, we've got to get ready for the party."

"Let's not start the day on the wrong foot, Harry." Greta didn't turn from chopping cottage cheese and chives into a skillet full of eggs.

"We killed a big lamb," Moe said. "It was full of guts like everybody else."

"Yuk—you're really on my case!" Penny scooted off toward the bathroom.

The morning of the Fourth Harry was up earlier than the sun. In the cool dawn, he put the sheep into their safe-pen, a small corral made of six-foot-high mesh, and he moved the colt into the stable where he could stay all day without harm.

He expected a lot of children, a lot of dogs, a few drunks, and some borderline cases, and he wanted them all to have a grand day.

By the time Harry returned, Greta was showing Moe the fine art of brushing his teeth. Moe didn't exactly care for the idea, but he was willing to try.

And then Harry recalled the little yellow Volkswagen wasn't parked outside. The cliff-hanging road became a menacing worry when someone didn't come home.

Greta was all adither, lost in anticipation of the party.

"Where can we put them all? I don't know what to wear— and all the ladies will look so nice . . ."

He put up the volleyball net in the pasture and pumped up the ball. He tried to show Moe the basics of horseshoe pitching but the shoes were heavy as sledgehammers and the boy needed more muscle on him before he could pitch that much iron forty feet.

The keg of beer chilled in an insulated box of crushed ice. Harry buried three quarts of his moonshine in the ice, and then started a fire in the old stone barbecue with oak branches for kindling. After the blaze was going good he dumped a wheelbarrow load of dry oakbark into the pit, bringing up a cloud of pungent smoke.

Gray-bearded Buzz Brown and broad-chested Frank Hodman, Harry's fishing cronies, arrived in a truck loaded with tables and benches.

After they'd set the tables out in rows radiating from the barbecue pit, he offered them a drink of the cold moonshine. As usual Frank refused. Frank had been born on the coast so long ago and was such a generous-hearted person everyone called the big man Uncle.

Buzz managed to tilt down three jolts of the clear corn liquor while bantering raucously about the foolishness of trying to bring Jim Goldfarb and Dorothy Staude together in this foothold on heaven, fantasizing them meeting in the green grass . . .

"And then, smitten with each other's few charms, despite their differing views on the minimum lot size, they fall in love and he leads her arm in arm in an iridescent bubble of joy to your hayloft where is conceived a sea otter that runs on manured methane!"

That was old grizzled Buzz.

"O shush up, Buzz, only thing you could get in the haymow would itch."

That was Uncle Frank.

After they left, Harry went to the swimming pool and switched on the filter. There were plenty of inner tubes and plastic floats.

He heard the Volkswagen come up the hill and quit worrying about Penny.

The coals were a fiery, flickering bed of heat radiating from the pit, and Harry's hands roasted as he fitted the loaded spit into its bearings.

He switched on the turning motor and waited through two revolutions to make sure the lamb was balanced and turning properly before going into the house for the marinade.

A blue Plymouth labored into the driveway and he went to welcome a small, middle-aged lady with long hair dyed the same color as the Pomeranian she carried in her left arm. Her face was heavily powdered, a futile try to hide withered-apple wrinkles.

"Hello, I'm Harry McAlister."

"Yes. I've seen you at the Post Office. I'm Polly Glendon. I live in the new house at Whispering Pines. Am I too early?"

"Not a bit. You're here, that's what counts."

He took her blue-veined hand and tried to make her believe he saw the beauty of twenty or thirty years ago.

"Why don't you come in and meet my wife and then later on I'll show you how the ranch works."

He led her into the house, through the gallery of blue-blazing Van Wingerdens. She stopped to look. She looked the bright colors up and down, not seeing them or the genius of draftsmanship.

"Nice," she said, and followed him into the kitchen.

Harry left her chatting with Greta. Before he could return to the spit, two more cars arrived.

The first dusty pick-up carried half a dozen kids and a dog that looked like a Doberman-husky cross. Lettered on the bumper in red and yellow paint was the name, Weird Harvest.

"Hello."

Harry shook the thumb of the tall gray-haired hippie, whose eyes were already stoned dead lightbulbs.

"Greetings and great energies on the occasion." Harvest spoke softly, insinuating words like a watersnake sneaking in the grass. "Meet our family—Morning Glory, Sunrise, Tender Fern, Waterfall, Meadow Morn, Frolic, and our dog, Peace-pipe, and my lady, Jonquil."

Harry greeted each of the standard hippie family, remembering that last year Harvest's father had bought them five acres and a pre-fab house and wrote them all off. They lived on welfare.

D.B. Darvey, with his wife and two kids, parked a red Cadillac in the driveway, and emerged empty-handed. Harry returned his big smile, but he wondered whether Greta had mentioned the potluck. So far he'd seen no one carrying the usual casserole or foil covered pan.

"Glad we could make it," Darvey said, his eyes hard to see behind dark, thick-rimmed glasses. A pencil and pen rode in the pocket of his tailored denim jacket, identifying him as a screen writer who commuted to Hollywood once or twice a week in his own plane. His wife shepherded the children to Harry, introduced them in a British accent, and he carefully shook hands with them. They didn't look much different than any other kids. The wife's name was Anna, and she'd just come from the beauty parlor, silken blonde hair precisely coiffed around her wide cheek bones.

Their big white standard bred poodle, as carefully groomed as Anna, strutted around.

Harry felt a twinge of premonition but the worry slipped by as more and more people arrived and hunted parking spaces.

Uncle Frank came alone this time with a big bowl of potato salad, and Harry asked him to handle the rest of the barbecue while he said hello to the guests and tried to prevent a traffic jam of incoming cars.

More people were arriving that he didn't know, and he tried to direct them into the house where Greta would show them around a little, but he was losing track. Whole families went by him as if he were a stranger.

The house yard where the beer and liquor were served filled up and overflowed out into the volleyball game. Twelve on each side. He hoped they'd let him play when he had time.

Margaret and Patti came in a jeep. He'd never learned their last names, but their ranchette down the road bore the carved sign: Pattimar.

Margaret moved like an army tank, drop-forged shoulder, howitzer neck, case-hardened jaw and armor piercing eyes. Patti played her opposite: pale, wispy, like a flame of burning alcohol, nearly invisible behind the dominant iron pig.

Harry shook hands and wished them a good day and complimented them on their two matched Afghans, beautifully groomed, whiskey colored dogs.

And he made a point of helping Amy Lou Robinson park in a protected space. She came from the car with a dignity that always uplifted his spirit. Her late husband had been a magazine editor, and she lived alone on her ranchette. Her fingers were knotted with arthritis and he took her hand as if it were a hummingbird.

Her crazy dog, a Dalmatian named Roger, hysterically leaped and bounded hither and yon, creating a chaos, but Amy Lou's serenity remained. She carried a flat loaf of Armenian pita.

"I was going to bring a green salad," she said, "but this bread is fresh and friendly, be sure to have a piece of it."

"I'll try, Amy Lou. You just go on into the kitchen. Greta is trying to organize the dinner from there."

Then, driving a Volkswagen bus, old Henry Giles and a friend arrived. Giles could have come in his 1929 Hispano Suiza, but no, today it's the VW bus day. An eccentric astronomer, he lived on a peak down the coast. Family had old Yankee money. He was smart enough not to keep a pet dog.

Right after Henry, Gary Phelps arrived. Harry's knowledge of Phelps came from the librarian who said he was a poet. Gary Phelps' neatly trimmed beard framed the awful erosion of his face. The drugs and battering he'd taken during his beatnik days marked him even to Harry's untrained eye. His poetry Harry had found to be obscure Zen, tripping through redwoods and south sea islands interchangeably.

But Harry was glad to shake the poet's hand and welcome him to the ranch. A lean, low-slung pit bulldog moved warily, checking the scene, tugging at his leash.

"Some road, man," Phelps said.

"I've been reading your work, Gary." Harry smiled so he'd know he wasn't picking on him. "It's hard going, too."

"The world is hard going. My asshole is hard going."

Harry guessed he'd been told off in a way. Phelps had established he was a tough sonofabitch.

Harry left him and his pit bull to greet Grant and Helen Wisenberg, the serigraphers who lived down the road.

Today they wore casual corduroys and flowered shirts. He shook Grant's hand first, and then took Helen's plump hand. Suddenly her mouth was locked on his. Her tongue ran in and out. Her eyes smouldered mischievously. With a fixed smile he numbly retreated to welcome somebody in a Porsche named Charles Howard, who turned out to be a movie star.

His boxer had a spike studded collar, and he himself looked distinguished in a linen coat and silk print ascot. Harry, still overwhelmed by Helen Wisenberg's assault and, hardly coherent, turned to greet Laurie Clements, the local grammar school teacher.

An automatic old maid, gaunt, high cheek bones, black, coarse hair, surely half Choctaw, Laurie was a reasonably competent teacher, and asked little enough from the community. Her police dog bounded out of the Plymouth, and with eyes alert, ears flared, he checked the area that had been marked and re-marked by twenty dogs already.

Families, perhaps doubled families that he had never seen before, ignored him and strolled across the driveway into the pasture, some smiling, some like dynamite ready to explode.

Buzz drove up in his old Ford, and as Harry was beginning to feel like a fish swimming upriver, Sam Hodman and his family arrived in their truck. A heavy bull of a man, the brother of Uncle Frank, Sam crushed Harry's hand.

Sam's big sunburned face grinned like a jack-o-lantern and he spoke in a reverberating voice deeper than bass. "Congratulations and commiserations for being born on the Fourth. Anybody that dumb deserves a goddamned kick in the butt." A rupture of laughter broke out of all of him, his broken and scarred massive hands, his thewed arms and tremendous chest. He was the irresistable Sam Hodman, neighbor, son of the son of earthy Big Sur.

Somewhere or sometime in the engulfing tide of people Harry suspected that instead of a party, he had an immigration on his hands, and when the skyrocket launched screaming into the sky, he thought: Gawdamighty!

Nobody could live in this fire prone country and be stupid enough to send flame off into the sky. Even as Harry ran to the happy fireworks group getting set to send up another flare, he saw that the first rocket had fallen into the lower irrigated pasture. Pure luck. Another ten feet and it would have landed in dry greasewood outside the fence and been on its way to burning everything.

By the time Harry reached the rocket launchers, Sam Hodman had planted his massive boots on the box of fireworks, glowering into the thin, dark face of a fullskirted lady Harry didn't know. A small boy clung to her left leg.

"That's the goddamnedest dumbest trick I've ever seen a hippie pull!" Sam was always direct.

"I want to teach my boy the old ways."

Her eyes were sullen, stubborn. Harry'd seen the same expression once on a she-bobcat that wouldn't back out of his chicken yard.

The crowd gathered around, adding grumblings and recriminations, mutters and murmurs.

"Lady, this party is to have fun and so everyone gets to know each other," Harry said. "Why don't you take the boy swimming?"

"You old chauvinist shit-ass," she said, and taking her boy's hand, turned away, then turned back for her last word. "I bought ten acres of this country, and it's just as good as yours, only mine is going to be liberated."

"By God, I hope you're downwind of me!" Sam's laughter sounded like a bass drum.

Greta tugged at Harry's arm. "There are children in the barn. One of them has cut his hand."

Jesus Christ! Why hadn't he locked that door?

Harry trotted through the swirling, calling people.

"Hey, Harry, you in for horseshoes?"

"Next game," he yelled over his shoulder, and worked his way through parked cars and a blue cloud of marijuana smoke, and made it to the open barn door where a gang of kids of all ages were playing cowboys and Indians with his hatchets, axes, froes, scythe, sickle. Even his giant broadaxe was being wielded by a boy hardly taller than its handle.

"Hey! Hey, kids!"

They stared at him with puzzled guilt. A few of them, strange youngsters, had the same dark feral quality of the skyrocket lady, the stubborn inverted righteousness that doesn't back down from even the obvious. They held their weapons like a painting of French peasants revolting. It occurred to him that they could kill and not even know what killing meant.

And he was glad Mohammed wasn't there.

"Easy, kids," Harry said gently. "Let's put all those tools back on the bench and go swimming. Someday you come up and I'll show you how to use them."

They stared at him. One little boy put his hatchet on the bench and ran outside screaming. The others moved quietly, keeping, he supposed, a sense of ego, tossing their implements to the concrete floor and stalking with a look of hate and outrage toward the open door.

"My dad said we could have fun up here," the last one, a tall, bleak-eyed boy said as he left.

Harry had no answer.

"Everybody out!" he yelled, just to be sure. "I'm locking the door."

He waited a couple seconds, heard nothing and pulled on the heavy door.

"Wait a minute, Pops."

Penny hustled down the ladder, straw stuck in the back of her waistband. In a second, Darvey, the screenwriter, hot and flushed, came after her.

"We've been looking at the old harness and traps and things," she said, her eyes set on Harry's forehead.

"That's one way to get straw up your ass," Harry said, sick and tired.

Darvey lumbered by. "Very interesting collection. Researching is half my business . . ." Muttering nonsense to cover his exit.

"Last call," Harry spoke into the quiet, hay smelling haven, pulled the door closed and snapped the padlock.

He had lost his smile.

Maybe he should have a drink and loosen up.

Working through the crowd to the box of ice, he managed to

get a paper cup half full of moonshine, and backed out again, all the time though, trying to introduce the different people, whether he knew them or not, to other people, talking about water systems, solar heaters, self sufficiency.

"Harry! Horseshoes!" He heard Johny Ripplewood call, and his soul was ready for the calm of the iron shoe pitch. On his way to the pits he noticed the late Hale peach tree had been stripped of fruit that would have ripened in another three weeks.

"Harry, the meat is nearly ready," Greta called.

Harry asked Buzz to help with the lamb.

They lifted it from the spit to a big piece of clean plywood on the picnic table, and as Harry carved, he noticed how little food was on the table.

"Greta, you'd better get the rest of the bowls and pans."

"That's all there is, Harry," she said, her smile unwavering, sending the message.

A line of hungry people with paper plates waited impatiently.

"Grab a piece, Buzz," Harry said, "there won't be enough."

"Women and children first," Buzz grinned.

"The hell with it," Harry said. "Let's have a beer."

Then he noticed Mohammed far down the line, alone and miserable.

"Moe," Harry called, "come on up here, I've saved a good bone for you." And he separated a riblet to put on the boy's plate.

"How come the coon goes first?" a tough little voice yelled.

Harry looked down the line carefully, trying to see someone to smash.

"Come on, Harry," Buzz said, "let's try the horseshoes."

He looked at faces, and all were still.

"Let's eat!"

Harry turned away with Moe. "You OK?" he asked.

"Sure," the boy answered. "You?"

Harry walked away to the horseshoe pits.

The volleyball game still went on, a flock of kids chased each other, the main company was all elbows at the food table, and like the children, dogs of every size and color were charging around across the pasture through the trees and back again.

Harry settled down, and took two horseshoes. His partner was a white-skinned real estate dealer named Funk. It didn't make any difference. Harry could win without him.

"Throw first, Harry, show us how to do it."

He hefted the heavy iron shoe, set his feet, straightened his back, loosened his shoulder, and stepped into the slow rhythm of the pitch. The shoe came up and he turned it as it left his hand. It sailed in a graceful arc, slowly making three quarters of a turn, and landed open faced against the steel peg, a perfect ringer. In the silence, he waited, set his feet and shoulders, and started the motion again with the second shoe, but he never threw it.

A sudden snarl and barking of savage dogs and an awful, piercing scream broke his rhythm.

Harry held, wheeled, and ran. Dodging through transfixed people as the razor sharp ululation rose and fell on the far side of the pasture, he guessed the dogs had a cat, rabbit or something, it might even be a child.

Why wasn't somebody doing something?

He ran hard and fast but the crowd, enthralled by a terrible moment, barred his way.

"Out of the way!" Harry yelled, and bulled through women and children.

"Hey! Watch out, old man!" he heard somewhere, but across the field something bloody was happening and being twisted into a soulshaking scream.

He fought into the inner ring, through packed people staring, immovable, transfixed spectators, and saw three dogs tearing a little orange furry thing that screamed and screamed and screamed.

Harry leaped into the tangle and with his left hand yanked at a collie, throwing him clear into the people and kicking and clubbing a boxer in the ribs with the horseshoe that had grown into his right hand, drove him snarling away, but the third dog, the heavy boned pit bull, had Polly Glendon's screaming Pomeranian in his locked jaws, and as Harry yelled and kicked at him, the dog only glowered and ground down all the harder, and Harry saw in those malevolent eyes, that stubborn brute force, the same eyes he'd been seeing all day and he heard the voices:

"Old chauvinist shit-ass . . ."

"Researching . . ."

"Greetings and great energies . . ."

"Coon . . ."

And without ever taking his own gaze from those sulfurous eyes, Harry swung the horseshoe as hard as he could and felt the skull crush, saw dog eyes turn to blue clay.

"Hey!"

Dead jaws still held their visegrip on the shrieking little dog, and as he smacked the pit bull again, more from a reflexive rage than anything else, the cry ended.

With both hands he pried the still stubborn jaws apart and laid the little dog out on the trampled grass, and tried to push some air into its torn lungs, but Polly Glendon's little Pomeranian was dead.

He looked up at the ring of staring faces. Jesus, he hated them.

Someone yelled, "Party's over, let's go down to the Inn."

No one said goodbye. They drifted away in dust.

Cars started, engines roared, and they were gone except for Buzz and Uncle Frank starting to clean up, Moe and Greta in the kitchen, and Polly Glendon, asleep on the couch in the sunroom.

2.

Coyote

Old Coyote calls from the ridge.
Old Coyote cries from his lonesome house.
His house is back in the back of the hills
In a little valley away back in the hills.

OCTOBER IS A time of distillation on Apple Pie Ridge. Cool but still summer dry, the wildoat covered hills tumble down to the sea like a great pile of polished brass pots. The air smells like an opened wine barrel, but sweeter and more pervasive, and a lavender haze veils the depths of the redwood canyons on either side.

October is a time for the farmer to count his harvest, a time for the craftsman to store his lumber, the beekeeper to protect his drowsy colonies, the housewife to make the end-of-the-garden pickles, the shepherd to tag his ram and ewes, the winemaker to rack his casks, the outdoorsman to roam his wilderness.

By the middle of the month, Harry had taken care of bees, poultry, lumber, sheep, gardens, orchard, and had racked the burgundy. He had nothing left on his mind except to hike the back country and absorb all the concentrated colors of the moody season.

Standing on a rocky crest high above his own ridge, he could see headland after headland facing the irrepressible western ocean, and the panorama of sunburnt hills, dark canyons, marble cliffs standing against an iron and flexing sea within the winey weight of the air lifted his old heart and distilled joy and wonder into a long widemouthed uninhibited howl: *"Hai Hai-ee!"*

Coming down at blue dusk, crossing a crackling knoll of dry grass, feeling full of time, Harry saw the old coyote, big as an Alsatian, trotting ahead of him. He stopped to make sure it wasn't a dog.

Against the great curve of purple light, Harry watched the coyote nose through mice dens, but he felt the coyote covertly watching him, studying his person, the inside maybe more than the outside, because Harry over the years had developed a superstitious awe of coyotes.

The Navajos made a two-faced god out of the unlikely coyote, the Trickster and the Creator, and old Harry knew he was a babe in the woods compared to the Indians.

"Ho, Grandfather," he said, starting off again with his long stork-legged gait, "I didn't mean to call you."

The big coyote, tail and head low, glanced at him and made a long circle around Harry as he hurried against the darkness that lifted from the canyon like a rising tide. The far sea held only splinters of light, and the single cloud on the horizon turned from pink to purple, casting a ghostly amethyst light on Harry's weather-worked face, the curious magical color of ocean mirrored at dusk, the hushed time, and he remembered October as the time of bonfires lighted back in the god-fearing hills of antiquity.

Harry lengthened his long stride, and concentrated on his footing, while the coyote seemed to make closer circles around his path, sometimes visible in a patch of reflected light, then gone, appearing and disappearing while at the same time gradually fading into the silent purple shadows.

And when he crossed through the fence that separated the

huge Ventana Wilderness from his own ranch, darkness hid the circling form, though Harry once saw a pair of glowing eyes.

"Stay over there, Grandfather, that land is yours," Harry said impulsively.

And to himself, he said, "Harry, you're getting senile, howling around in the hills, talking to ghosts."

When he reached the permanent pastures and outbuildings surrounding his house, he heard Billy, the colt, nicker, and he smelled sweet oak smoke coming from the chimney. A little fire seemed natural in the fall.

As he opened the front door, he thought that maybe he and Greta had lived so long and so close to the wilderness that they were becoming more real than rational, more Indian than Yankee, that they had finally adapted to the hard excesses of nature.

He smelled dinner on the stove, and called ahead to avoid startling her, "Hey, Greta, you to home?"

"No, sweetie," she called back, giggling, "nobody to home 'ceptin' us chickens."

October and the hills had grabbed her too.

He swatted her haunch as he passed, and reached for the jug of moonshine.

"You're late," she murmured, concentrating on slicing an onion.

"I went clear to the top. The colors are so rich now, the maples and the sycamores, and the poison oak is bright as blood."

"We should press apples tomorrow, " she said. "The wine-saps are starting to fall."

"Fine with me."

He sipped the clear liquor and felt the fire roll down his throat. It tasted of corn and sugar. You could light a spoonful and it would burn with a flickering blue flame, and you could cook a cup of soup on it or singe a bird, or run a car on it, but he had made it to drink, and in a minute the probing ache in his hips would dissolve.

"Lambshanks for dinner," she said.

"Plenty of bay leaf?"

"Pipe down. I am the cook," she smiled, her strange old-young Laplander features flushed from the heat of the stove and the love of the doing.

"I should have brought an armful of that poison oak, so crimson, it looks like fire on the mountain, just masses of flame on the ridges and headlands."

"I appreciate your leaving it in its proper habitat," she laughed. "I saw the sun sparkle on Piper Point just as it set, and good heavens, that's twenty miles up the coast!"

The kitchen steamed with the redolence of freshly pickled zucchini and braised lamb trotters simmering in buttery to-mato sauce.

During dinner he told her about the coyote.

"Coyotes are two-faced," she commented. "I almost cry when they howl at the moon, but still the coyote is sneaky."

"Seems like they want to test man all the time, see what he's made of."

"You'd better take your shower right away," she inter-rupted his musing. "The meeting starts at eight."

"I'm tired," Harry protested. "Nobody will listen to us anyways."

"Nevertheless," she was firm, "maybe we can save some-thing for the children."

He dressed in a clean flannel shirt and Levis and a soft sweater Greta had knitted from natural lambswool, and he drove the old truck down the switchbacks into the pitchblack and wet mouldering valley.

The old community hall that Harry had helped shingle thirty years ago stood in a grove of redwoods alongside the Big Sur River which in October became hardly more than a small creek babbling over quartz cobbles.

In the nearly full hall, he found Sam Hodman had saved them two chairs. Big and with a voice like a freight train, Sam Hodman was comfortable to sit by unless you disagreed with him.

"Who's running this show, Sam?" Harry asked.

"That bastard Darvey. Nobody elected him to anything, he just appointed himself the Master."

"He must have the votes then or he wouldn't bother."

"If you didn't know him, you'd believe he was more interested in preserving the natural coast than in building up Daniel Boone Darvey." Sam's bitter laughter boomed like a pipe organ through the buzzing hive.

"I had a coyote walk down from the summit with me this evening, tame as pie."

"You should have shot the sonofabitch and hung him from your fence."

"He wasn't hurting anything."

Before Sam could respond, D.B. Darvey rose from a table on stage where two other men and a woman sat with notebooks, tape recorder, and ballpoint pens, looking serious and dedicated.

Darvey took off his heavy-rimmed glasses and held them toward the light, but his bulging pig eyes needed to be obscured and the gesture ended with the glasses promptly back in place.

The hall hushed as he cleared his throat, stood on his toes, squared his shoulders, and announced with a broadlipped smile, "Ladies and gentlemen, neighbors and friends, lend me your fears." A titter of laughter responded on cue like a canned laugh-track. "We're keeping it simple tonight. The Coastal Commission on Land Use wants community input, specifically on the problem of density. Will someone speak to the subject?"

"What's the matter with the way it is right now?" Sam Hodman roared.

Gary Phelps, the slender, bearded poet, rose from his chair at the table, and spoke softly, "Because the zoning now is a five acre minimum lot, making a potential of twenty-three-thousand lots available in this area." He read from a typed page, his voice mild, reasonable, semi-holy. "Now that's about fifty times the dwellings already here and there is considerable community agreement that we have already reached maximum density possible without erosion of our natural lifestyle, the organic society we all came here originally for . . ."

Harry let the reformed beatnik grind out his rhetoric, until Greta whispered in his ear, "You'd better speak up, Harry, they're going to rob the kids for sure."

" . . . suggest and so formally move that we adopt a forty acre minimum lot size for single family dwellings . . ."

"Wait a minute," Harry hated to stand and address an audience, knowing already how inept and incoherent he sounded, "just a second there, Mr. Volunteer Chairperson, first of all, there ain't enough water right now for all the new folks. The first two year drought we have, you'll find that out. And then you'll all be for dammin' up the river."

"That's pure prejudice," the lady at the table retorted quickly.

"No, ma'am," Harry flushed, "I'm trying to tell you that if you'll just live with nature's laws, you won't have to make density laws. The only way to beat all the outsiders' big money pressure is to have a Federal umbrella, but if I was to vote for a forty acre minimum that won't never hold up against the big subdividers' plans, I'd like to make it retroactive about twenty years. That was a mighty harmonious density then."

A cold silence lay over the hall, until Sam Hodman growled like a foghorn, "You tell 'em, Harry."

"I've been to a lot of meetings in this building," Harry peered around the room at the strange and dedicated faces, "but I hardly know any of you by first name. That's tragic in this country."

Darvey tapped his gavel politely, "Did you have an amendment to the motion, Mr. McAlister?"

"No, I'm discussing it, Mr. Darvey," Harry answered, flushing a deep red. "What's your hurry?"

"No hurry." Darvey smiled tolerantly, nodding, demonstrating to the audience that they should give the old goat his due.

Harry caught the meaning of that nod, the insult, but Greta

pressed his hand. "I'd like to tell you I promised my kids that when they come back they will each have a homesite on our seventy-five acres. If you make it a forty acre minimum, they can't have their inheritance. I'd like the motion to read that anybody with twenty years residency may divide his ranch for his children."

"That's a loophole a speculator could drive a subdivision through," Darvey said quickly.

"But you're really turning the coast over to the big corporation hotels," Harry responded.

The house vote passing the forty acre minimum without exception took about one more minute.

Home safely, Harry lay unsleeping in bed, his long body rigid with anger, and he felt like crying for the losing of his good dream. Greta patiently patted his bony shoulder until he slept.

In the morning after chores, Harry let his anger loose. "Christ almighty, we built this farm from a rockpile! We built it ourselves, with our own bloody hands because we didn't have nothing else!"

"You'll bust into kindling wood if you don't bend some, Harry." Her patient tone ran him out of the house.

Still steaming, he walked the lower fields of the ranch, checking the sheep and the avocado orchard. There were only twenty trees, but he had grafted especially strong producing scions from other trees on the coast into his trees tripling the number of varieties. Usually he could pick up half a dozen ripe avocados fallen to the grass.

He found four freshly skinned seeds.

Goddamn coons, eating my best avocados.

He walked around the woven wire fence until he found the hole.

A big animal had dug and bellied under the tight mesh. The hairs caught in the wire were brown and coarse.

Coyote. That sonofabitch thinks I adopted him. Well, Grandfather, I'm sick of you already.

In the barn he found a length of piano wire. He bent an eye in one end of the wire and went back to the orchard fence where he spread a loop carefully around the hole. If the coyote stuck his head in that snare, he would not only strangle to death, he'd likely cut his head off, too.

That night he told Greta about the missing fruit and the snare, and she said, "Harry, you're still upset about the meeting. Maybe you ought to just fix the fence."

"He'd dig in someplace else."

Before breakfast, he made his rounds, dawdling, enjoying the crispy air, the fine noises of small wakening birds and bugs.

He hoped the snare would be empty. The pink lighted, frisky morning was too grand to share with violent death.

He found no torn up ground, no stiffening carcass. The thin wire was simply turned at right angles to the hole. Maybe coyote nosed it out, but he suspected Greta might have come out in the night and turned the wire.

No way of knowing. Best forget it.

He picked three freshly fallen avocados from the dewy grass and brought them into the kitchen where Greta in her robe was baking Swedish pancakes.

"Missed him. Old Grandfather is too smart for me." Harry watched her face.

"He probably knows how you feel now." She blushed.

"You're crazy," Harry laughed. "Nicely crazy."

After breakfast, he went to the barn and dragged the cider press outside. Washing the dust off it, he heard a Volkswagen perking up the hill and felt an automatic twinge of fear and remorse. Why should he always think it was Penny coming again?

But at the thought of his eldest daughter, he felt his deepest emotions shift formation, sending in the defense, armoring up, goal line stand, rooting in the bottom of the bag for coyote answers, honest and foolish, sensible and silly.

He backed into the darkness of the barn where he could observe the driveway. If she were alone or had brought another odd-ball along, he'd just hide out until she left. But if she brought Moe, he'd welcome them.

The yellow bug pulled up the front driveway and Penny

climbed out of the driver's side, her long black hair loosely framing fine and lovely features.

The other door slowly opened, and Harry let his breath out in pleasure when the small dark-skinned boy emerged, yawned, scratched at his wooly head, and looked about with wide curious eyes.

Harry hurried out to the car, put an arm around Penny, felt her quick peck on his cheek, and looked a moment at her face.

No bruises, only tiny wrinkles netting her dark blue eyes and her mouth was changing to a downward slant, making her smile upside down.

"Hi, Pops," she said. "Here's that little old bad penny popping up again."

"Hush that. You'll get it together soon enough."

Before she could respond he turned and hoisted his grandson high, held him up at arm's length for a brief second, and then dropped him to his chest and hugged him hard. "Good to see you, Moe."

The round dark eyes looked into his. "How is the horse, Grandpa?"

They sat at the table while Greta happily put out mugs and plates, and talked of the weather and cars while Moe munched a cookie and drank a glass of milk. When he was nearly finished, Penny said, "Why don't you run outside, Moe. Go look at a horse or something."

The bite was coming, Harry realized. Not that money meant so much, only this attacking ritual had a deeper meaning he couldn't understand.

"I've got a chance at a really neat job in Las Vegas . . . no, no, don't freeze up . . ."

"How much?" Harry asked.

"Like you don't want Moe living in a slum, do you?" Penny retorted. "Besides, you spent a bundle sending the boys to college, and I never got any of that."

"The boys wanted to learn," Harry said. "And your little sister wanted to get married."

"And so now they're all fifteen thousand miles away."

"It's never too late to go to school, girl," Greta said.

"You could leave Moe here until you're settled," Harry added.

"Is that a condition of the loan?" Penny's smile reminded Harry of a sand shark.

"I'll write you a check." Greta went to Harry's walnut desk.

What a waste, he thought. What a sick tragedy racked out of an obsolete teeny-bopper, and he went outside and walked toward the horse pasture where he could see the little boy leaning against the broad chest of the colt. Just leaning, dreaming, soaking in the smooth body warmth of the horse.

"Next year you can ride him, Moe. You can race your shadow."

"Would he be mine?" he said at last.

"If it looked like you two belonged together, I sure wouldn't get in the way."

A screeching yip from across the canyon like a piercing demand for inclusion interrupted their talk.

Harry pointed out the brown form standing on a great contoured rock. Its rough tawny coat caught the sun and its strong stance was perfectly animal against the granite.

"A dog?" Moe whispered.

"Coyote. He's been hanging around, probably getting too old to hunt."

"What does he eat?"

"About anything from a grasshopper to a sheep."

"Moe!" Penny called from the house. "Hurry it up, chop-chop, we're on our way."

Moe clutched the colt's leg, holding harder.

"Guess we better mind," Harry said. "There'll be another day."

Moe took his warped and calloused hand and said, "Someday Billy and I will go riding in the hills."

"Sure. You bet."

They walked slowly back to the driveway where Penny revved the yellow bug impatiently.

He kissed the boy's dark cheek and shook hands with him

man to man, and went to Penny's open window and let her peck his eroded cheek again. "Lots of luck, child."

"Sure, Pops," she smiled upside down again.

"Penny," he said suddenly, "we don't want to take the boy away from you, but a little settling down wouldn't hurt him none."

"OK, Pops, I'll think about it." She put the car in gear. In a minute they were gone, leaving only the caustic reek of exhaust fumes.

That night from the ridge above came the strident cry, an eerie repetitive lament, the world's anguish concentrated into the voice of the coyote, like the last Jew on earth singing his faith and woe to heaven.

Harry went outside to wonder if there were a secret message, a key to the universe in that ululation, and he remembered in the cool moonlight when once there were packs of coyotes on the ridges reaching each other with their concerts, and other times when the lions cried sadly in the night, and foxes coughed and barked. Where was all the game going? What had happened to drive away the lions and foxes and coyotes? Of course he had driven them off his small homestead and fenced them out. But except for a few deer, he hadn't hunted the wildlife, had killed only what his family needed to eat. And he'd never permitted his guard dogs to run off the ranch.

What is this lament, Grandfather? You have a hill and all the night.

Toward the end of the week, Penny called collect.

"Pops," her voice came through giggly, stoned, "here's the bad penny again."

"What's the trouble?"

"The rent's due, the job fell through, my car blew, and Moe needs new shoes!"

"Honey, cash money's hard to come by around here."

"And my teeth hurt and I want to go to New Orleans."

"Jesus Christ," he groaned, "you can't take Moe to New Orleans."

"Can you wire me six hundred?"

He took a while to think. She'd already wiped out the checking account.

"Pops," she said, "make it five. I'll get it right back to you."

"What about Moe?"

"You want my little pickaninny for collateral?"

"How can you take him south?"

"All right," she said, "drive a hard bargain, but just till I'm back on my feet."

Next morning early he made the trip to town, tapped the savings account, and after lunch, waited at the bus station, quietly observing the passing parade of travelers, bizarre to his countryman's eyes... an ancient Chinese lady, many quiet field hands, a group of chattering whores dressed outrageously, a crippled Mexican, a junky panhandler... mainly they were blacks and browns. The poor, he decided. They can't afford to fly and the trains don't run anymore. Within that seething waiting room was the beating heart of a revolution. The sooner the better, he decided. I'll help pull on the rope...

A loudspeaker announcing the bus arrival interrupted his reverie. He stood slack shouldered by the doorway and waited as incoming passengers passed by. Odd, he thought, there are no happy faces, but at the airport, folks look kind of cheerful.

Finally, at the end of the line, little Moe, still wearing a cardboard sign saying MONTEREY CAL pinned to his sweater, came trudging along carrying a big brown paper bag. He looked as depressed as everyone else, eyes dull, head down, shufflling along.

"Moe!"

The little boy looked up, his amber eyes firing a smile that lighted his dark features.

"Grampa!"

"He your kin?" a rotund black man grinned.

"Sure is!" Harry knelt to give Moe a long hug.

"How is the horse?" Moe asked.

On the way down the coast, chugging along in the old truck, Harry mentioned the various scenic landmarks, Point Lobos like a stranded whale, Hurricane Point diving into the sea, and coming across the Little Sur River he pointed inland toward the high razorback of gray limestone called Pico Blanco. Then the massive sea stack of Point Sur, and the dark river valley, and the turn off through the subdivision named Estates Del Sur, and on up the mountainside into the sun of Apple Pie Ridge and home.

"Here we be, Moe," Harry switched off the key. "Old Apple Pie."

"Am I going to stay?"

"Don't worry, Moe," Harry said quietly, "we'll have us a good old time."

After the chores and dinner, Greta announced bedtime. "Maybe tomorrow night I can sleep with the horse," Moe told Greta as she tucked him in.

"Sure," she laughed, and kissed him goodnight.

In the early morning before anyone else was awake, Harry made his rounds from pen to pen, feeding and watering, making sure all was well with the ranch population. The morning air tasted of orange autumn, and maples flamed across the canyon. The sea lay like grape jelly and the high pastures, tawny as lion skins, glowed in the first sun.

At first he thought it was a deer crossing one of those bright sunny patches on the upper slope, but as his eyes adjusted to the range, he saw the unmistakable tail of the old coyote, the sore footed pace, the sharp nose in the morning air.

Jumping to a limestone crag, the coyote stopped to survey his domain.

Harry felt a nervous quiver run up his spine.

"Listen here, Grandfather," Harry muttered, "better you travel on and leave me alone."

Unhearing, uncaring, the coyote savored the breeze, leaped stiffly off the crag to the grassy hillside and trotted on, disappearing in a patch of darkness.

"You keep pushing on me, coyote, I'm going to pop you off," Harry said aloud, and catching himself, self-consciously added, "Crazy as a hoot owl, old man."

The sheep drowsed in a patch of gnawed and broken mesquite, but they came running when he dumped a bucket of
bruised apples over the fence. Like autumn, they were suspended in their function, resting between birth and breeding.
As soon as the nights grew a little colder, Mac would cover the
ewes, and start the clock to ticking again.

At the henhouse, something jarred his mood. The hens
were too scattered to count. Their fence was tight, and the few
feathers loose on the ground only meant they were starting to
molt. Yet something troubled him, and he inspected the mesh
fence again. The cement lined irrigation ditch that passed
under the fence ran full of water and all seemed secure.

Next day he and Moe tried to count the loose hens, and they
kept coming up short.

Greta laughed at him. "You're getting to be as bad as a
mother hen yourself."

"Something's wrong up there." He was annoyed with himself more than anything. "Maybe a bobcat or coon has found a
way into the chicken house."

"Maybe it's a snake," Moe said.

"Snake couldn't get out with a chicken."

That night Harry took the flashlight and counted the hens
asleep on the roost. Thirteen and two roosters. Five plump
layers had disappeared into thin air.

He kept them locked inside and counted them again the
next night. Another hen gone.

Next morning he and Moe studied the concrete ditch that
carried creek water not only to the chickens but on to the
orchard below.

"Moe, some damned varmint is swimming underwater into
the pen."

"Maybe a beaver."

"Beaver don't eat chickens."

"What is it then?"

"Coon, fox, probably coyote."

"Grandpa," the boy hesitated, "is 'coon' a bad name?"

Shaken, Harry waited a moment. "It's an old racist insult

that only ignorant bullies use. But really a coon is one hell of a smart and handsome creature."

"I'm not a coon." Moe smiled shyly. "I'm a man."

Harry found a dusty #2 steel trap in the barn. He planted both feet on the springs, opened the jaws, flipped the tongue over into the notch of the pan, and gently took his weight off the springs.

"Now, Moe, that's a dangerous instrument, all set to go off. You never want to touch the pan with your hand or foot." Harry tapped the pan with a stick. The trap jumped as steel jaws snapped together, chopping the stick in two.

Moe jumped in fright. "Won't it hurt him?"

"That's what he has to suffer for stealin' chickens."

"We got to catch him." Moe was determined again.

Harry reset the trap and placed it in the slow flowing ditch just under the fence. He hooked the chain into the mesh and hid its loose links with a few leaves.

Satisfied, Harry said, "That's it, boy. It'll drown him."

"Suppose he has babies at home?"

"Moe, I don't like this any better than you do."

"Maybe we could put some kind of wire in the ditch so he can't get through."

"Then if it plugs up, the whole yard floods." Harry knew he wasn't telling the whole truth.

He had decided the coyote was pushing on him, taunting and crowding, nibbling away at the ranch like his do-gooder neighbors, nibbling away at his own person, like his daughter.

Good God Harry thought with a curious sense of surprise, *I have become the ranch, I am an institution disintegrating.*

They walked on down to the meadow on the point where they sat in the tall dry grass, watching the Cheviots browse on the hillside below, big fat panting puffs of wool.

Harry knew the coyote would show himself again, and as they lounged in the brittle grass, he watched the surrounding slopes until his roving eye caught the dull tan coat in the matching grass just over the protective fence, a hundred feet away.

"There he is, Moe," Harry whispered.

Harry looked into the old coyote's wily eyes, and wondered at the two-faced Trickster legends, the miracles, the cunning, the creation, the obscene vulgarities heaped on this animal as he now extended his front legs forward, and bowed his head upon them, his brushy tail standing in a high curl, his golden eyes never changing.

"He's lonesome," Moe said.

The tail wagged in a friendly appeal.

"No, coyote," Harry said, "you stay back on your ridge where you belong."

The gray-muzzled coyote cocked his fluted ears a moment as if asking for the message to be repeated, but Harry had said it clear enough, and in another retreating moment he was gone in the tall grass.

That night at dinner, Harry didn't mention the trap, and Moe busily discussed the merits of a warm bath over a warm shower with Greta. Maybe it wasn't wise to bypass Greta, but he remembered the snare turned aside, and thought if she'd let him catch the predator then, there would be six more hens in the chicken house now.

Still, what were six stupid chickens against the life of the wise old coyote? You could sacrifice six hens to a strange idol and feel all the better for it. And maybe it was a coon or a fox taking the hens.

That was a handsome coyote. A big male who in a way was trying to tell him something, and he in his own way was trying to tell the coyote something, and maybe nobody would learn anything, or maybe they would all learn a lot, depending, he supposed, upon whether anyone really cared about learning anything anyway.

Damn it, the trap was on his conscience. He debated with himself by the fire before going to bed, and once again he had to conclude his duty was to the hens.

But he waited in the morning for Moe, and he made himself go slow. He put Moe up on the colt's back and steadied him there for a minute or two, and he wandered about looking at the dry brush and smelled the blooming lemon trees, until

Moe impatiently urged, "Come on, Grandpa, let's see what we caught."

The brown form in the water lay still as they approached.

"What is it, Grandpa?"

Harry hated himself. He tasted acid in his throat. "It's Grandfather coyote."

The chain was pulled tight, and as they came closer, they could see the coyote had used all the chain and stretched the full length of his body to keep his head above water. His cloudy eyes were open, his muzzle grizzled and silver, his teeth worn.

"He's alive!" Moe whispered.

"Hello, Grandfather," Harry said. "You are caught in my chicken house."

The coyote, fully extended, made no response. The effort to keep his nose above water all night had exhausted him.

"All I have to do is hit him with a rock." Harry picked up a rock the size of a baseball. "Just bash his head in."

"Don't, Grandpa!"

"Hear that, you old bastard? A little boy begs for your life," Harry yelled furiously.

The coyote's expression never wavered, his whole being intent on just breathing.

"No, Grandpa."

"Don't worry, child," Harry muttered, "I don't have it in me to hate so much. But he may be hell turning loose."

"Why?"

"Because that sonofabitch can bite through a leg bone if he wants."

"But he wouldn't bite you —"

"Would you savage me?" Harry saw nothing in the old eyes, only a will to live, nothing vicious nor frenzied, only resignation to a sickening time.

> *In my house, you, Coyote,*
> *In my trap, you, Coyote,*
> *What are you doing?*
> *Go back to your house in the hills.*

Harry unwired the chain, and dragged the big coyote out

from under the mesh and saw the ratty tail and wet ribs and the scrape on the ankle where the coyote had pulled the trap clear down to his toes, gaining the two inches he needed to breathe through the night.

"Poor old boy, he's pretty near paralyzed," Harry said. "Been locked in the same position so long."

"Is it bad?" Moe whispered.

"It's good for me. I don't think he's got any fight left."

Harry turned the trap so he could get his weight on the springs, letting the jaws drop open.

"Pull his leg out of there, Moe," he said.

Moe didn't move. The trap lay open, but Harry couldn't reach down to remove the leg.

"I'm scared."

"Scared? So what? You still have to pull his leg out!"

Moe moved slowly closer, his eyes big and round.

"Go ahead, boy. You've got the guts to touch an animal."

"Yessir," Moe said and at arm's length with gentle fingers, he lifted the paw out of the open steel jaws.

The coyote lay inert, exhausted, shivering, soaked, and only the phosphor of his eyes showed he lived.

"Why don't he run away, Grandpa?"

"Pooped out. Arthritis locking his joints." Harry stepped off the trap. "You could kiss him right now and he wouldn't care."

"Boy, he's lucky."

"Look here, *Viejo*," Harry dangled the trap before the unwavering golden eyes, "from now on you stay on your side of the fence."

"He's going to die," the little boy said.

"Everybody's against him, but coyotes endure."

Moe found a grain sack in the chicken house and toweled the gaunt animal's pelt until the coyote slowly tucked his legs up close to his body.

"Mr. Coyote," Moe said, "you're a good old boy but you mustn't eat our chickens anymore."

The coyote slowly lowered his head and closed one eye.

3.

Lion in the Rain-Rinsed Morning

BY THE TIME Harry finished his coffee, a pale pearl of light silhouetted the eastern peaks. Even in the mists of deep winter the light warmed his spirit and put his thoughts on discovery and freedom.

While wife, hens, colt, sheep slept, he felt renewed and released in that private hour of bridging daybreak.

Outside in the drizzly first light, the tall man stopped to take a deep breath, savoring the freshness of cold and pristine mountain air, and habitually waited for Peppy, the dun colored feist, and Poky, the old black Lab, to join him on his rounds.

When they didn't arrive, he went to the barn alone. The dogs were probably teaming up on a coon or bobcat. Peppy, being small and nosy, guarded the homestead by calling in the big Lab whenever she needed help.

The dogs didn't meet him at the barn. He forked hay into the colt's corral, and waited again. But after feeding cats, chickens, and the two feeder pigs, he knew the foot-loose and free-born morning was out of joint.

He whistled and called at every pen, but the dogs never came.

Maybe the rain after such a long dry spell had changed their ways.

"Here, Poke! Here, Pep!" he called, a sense of black dread rising like bitter sap in his blood.

The wet morning seemed so empty without them nosing ahead of him, marking every jurisdictional sign along the way.

In the kitchen, Greta in her old woolen robe, folded grated cheese and tomatoes into an omelette.

"Dogs are gone," Harry said.

"They'll turn up okey-dokey." Greta put toast and the divided omelette on hot plates and brought them to the table.

Harry idly wondered why her long red hair had no gray in it. His own mop was snow white.

"This morning everything seemed to be opening up, but now I feel like I'm being choked down like a wild horse."

"Eat your breakfast," she laughed. "You always get cabin fever about the first of the year."

"By God, we been married too long when you've got my moods figured out according to the seasons." He smiled.

"I'll never figure you out," Greta shook her head. "Never. You're a strange one."

"Bosh," he said, rising and putting his empty plate in the sink. "I'm just a man earning his independence." He went outside, the dogs on his mind.

Dim sun filtered through the overcast, and a light breeze came from the south signaling more rain.

"More the better," he muttered. "Bring it on."

"Who you talking to?" he asked himself whimsically. "You giving orders to the weather boss now?"

He whistled and called, "Here, Poke! Here, Pep!"

They were too old to stray or get stranded on a cliff. He knew they were dead.

The only way they'd die would be protecting some part of the ranch. Only the livestock this time of year needed protection. Colt was OK. Pigs OK. That left sheep.

He rambled through a hillside pasture until he found the Cheviots resting on a rocky slope. He counted five ewes and

Mac, the ram, and four yearlings. They were placid lumps of gray wool melting into the mountainside. He could see nothing nervous or disturbed about them, yet he felt a fear like burning ice in that tranquil, drowsing flock.

"Goddamn you dumb sonsabitches," he accused them bitterly. "What happened to my dogs?"

The sheep lifted their grave, biblical heads an inch.

He walked an expanding circle through grass and mesquite trying to cover the hillside in a terrible search. He slipped on slick ledges and tripped over greasewood branches, but he was thorough.

Occasionally he stopped to call, "Here, Poke! Here, Pep!" but after awhile it became a meaningless exercise. The wet brush soaked his clothes and soon only his feet were dry. He carried no fat on his bony frame to keep out the cold.

"Here, Poke! Here, Pep!"

He thought he heard a sound, not really dog or bird, but some discord outside the tranquil harmony of the hillside. Quail called. The breeze whispered in the brush. A junco hopped. But the sound he thought he heard wasn't right with them.

"OK, dog," he said aloud. "I'm coming."

"Here, Poke, here, Pep," he called, trying to zero in on that odd noise.

Again an indistinct whimper.

He cranked his aching hips up the hill to the hogback and on toward the last fence where the dripping brush grew like a jungle over his head.

His mind was bent on the dogs and he never really thought about the cold and the wet. He was, if anything, more worried about whether his knotted joints would make him scream from driving them up the hill.

"Goddamn you hips, cut this meanness out!" he groaned, staggering now and breathing hard as he reached the ridgeback that flattened out into a small bench covered with soft green lupine.

The ground was ripped and the brush torn. He saw tracks of

his dogs in the wet earth and the tracks of a great cat.

"Oh boy," he moaned. Too big a cat. Too big.

Poky, old, gray-muzzled Lab, lay where the lion had dropped her. He saw the wide spacing of the fangs that had driven into her brain. Her neck was broken. The cat had simply grabbed old Poky by the head and shook her a couple times and dropped her. No doubt Peppy had nipped his ass, and he had turned to swat Pep like a baseball. Home run.

"You sonofabitch," he growled, hating and swearing revenge even before he found the little brown dog tangled in a clump of brush where she'd fallen.

Alive. Barely. A lot of bones broken. One smack of a clubbing forepaw in the ribs. A mess. Harry took his wet shirt off, looking into the worried brown eyes of the little dog.

"This is going to hurt some, Pep, but it's all there is."

He slid the shirt under the dog and tied sleeves and tail together, making a compact package, and bare-chested, he lifted the silent animal in his corded arms and carefully made his way back to the house.

Peppy didn't whimper, but her bug eyes never left his face.

He'd have to kill the cat.

Yet mountain lions were already decimated by forest fires and trophy hunters. Always the goddamned riddle. Right and wrong. Kill or be killed. Lion, why didn't you stay back in the wilderness where you belong? He'd said the same thing to every other animal that had challenged his farmstead and his way of living. And old Poke was a part of him. Stiff and bloody, she'd been his companion eleven years. And Peppy'd come along eight years ago. They'd paid their dues. The lion to Harry was a stranger, an abstract that he had not even seen, let alone touched or fed or cared about.

"Oh boy," he muttered miserably as he went into the house.

Greta was kneading new bread dough because it was Tuesday. She turned pale when she saw her grizzled, rope-muscled husband enter the kitchen with the shirt-wrapped parcel in his hands.

"Peppy," he said. "Damned lion tagged her."

"O God, Harry, you look awful. You OK?"

"I'm OK," he said, stripping wet boots, socks and dungarees off pale blue legs. "I got a heater in the truck."

"Have a drink," she said.

"I will," he said going into the bedroom and emerging in clean, dry clothes moments later.

He drank half a glass of his clear moonshine in one swallow.

"Good stuff," he said quietly.

"Poky?"

"Dead." He set his jaw, wanting to curse the lion he meant to kill. "Up on the hill. I'll fetch her down when I get back."

He took the little dog to the truck, fitted her into a cardboard box on the floor and drove on down the hill.

"Don't give up, Pep," he said. "We don't ever give up, you know. If we can't feel better, at least we hang on."

The small, bald man in a smock touched the little dog's body and shook his head. "It would be very expensive to save her. I'd suggest we put her to sleep."

Harry's shoulders sagged as he felt a burden too heavy to bear but he considered the decision as dispassionately as he could, and finally replied, "No, sir, if she'd done something like gettin' run over by a car, I'd maybe say yes, but she was doin' her job, and I'm not goin' to kill her for that. I want you to do your best."

The vet smiled. "I like a man to tell me what he wants."

Peppy disappeared into the surgery, and Harry walked up and down the sidewalk, trying to keep his thoughts on the little dog's recovery, but the dark image of a maul-fisted mountain lion rode his mind.

He was already engaged in a battle with a berserk cat gone off its range, attacking the ranch dogs, the ranch, himself.

He didn't see the morning traffic, and he didn't smell the poisonous air, nor hear the spewing, ripping trucks moving from market to market, the moil of trade.

The little man in his smudged smock caught him as he passed.

"Mr. McAlister, she's still alive. I've splinted the fractures and put her in a body cast."

"Can I take her home?"

"Maybe next week."

"Hell." Harry frowned.

"What exactly happened?"

"Damned mountain lion nailed her. I'm goin' to have to kill him."

"It's none of my business, Mr. McAlister," the small vet said, "but there's a law against killing mountain lions."

"If that lion comes against me on my own land, I don't need the State to solve my problem."

"I'd keep it quiet."

"I'll be in tomorrow to look at Peppy," Harry said. "I thank you for any extra attention she gets. Takes some nerve for a little dog to fight a cat ten times her size."

Harry drove back down the coast highway, going his usual safe and sane forty-five miles an hour, enraging the speeders bottled up behind him. He ignored the line of cars and the insults they yelled when they passed on treacherous curves. He liked to look at the cliffs and the blue and white sea bashing against them.

The sea must win against the rock because the sea has the energy of the outer world tides, but then the rock in a thousand years is renewed by the energy cooking inside the earth. Interesting balance, the magma core of the earth against the pull of the dead moon.

And the speeding cars raced against a clock he couldn't understand. He'd driven the cliff-hanging highway forty years and never had had an accident, and yet every day the ambulances howled and the tow trucks pulled crumpled cars back up the cliffs. What kind of an independent clock does Death have, and when does it start to tick?

He stopped at the Post Office and mentioned the lion's assault to the Postmistress, but he put no importance on what he said or who heard it.

At home, Greta buttered a heel of hot fresh bread for him and poured him a glass of cold metheglin. He watched in admiration for a moment. Her long red hair, her tanned face marked by the wrinkles of an easy smile. All you need to live forever is a good heart and the love of life, he thought.

The fragrant mead he'd made last year from extracted honey-combs suited his mood, calming, restoring, enhancing the sense of his own person in his own place.

After I bury old Poke, I'll bring the sheep into the front pasture," he told her.

He spent the rest of the day digging a good deep grave on a knoll overlooking redwood groves and the sea below.

He didn't linger or sentimentalize. Poky was old and had lived better than most dogs.

His sheep, the slim-ankled, small, clean faced Cheviots, were prime targets for a crazy lion. The field that served in summer for baseball, horseshoes or volleyball lay next to the house, and the sprinklers had kept the grass up.

He opened interlocking gates to drive the five old ewes and four young ones and old Mac into the pasture. He doubted if the lion would be crazy enough to come into the front yard.

The sheep had no fear, only an insatiable appetite to graze on the new grass. The old ewes were due to lamb in a few weeks if Mac had covered them well. They usually dropped twins.

While he was filling the woodbox at day's end, the phone rang and his caller identified herself as Mrs. Hugo Byrd. Her voice came over crisp and strong.

"I understand you have a lion problem. Have you called the Fish and Game?"

Harry tried to keep his composure. "No, ma'am."

"I've had a heavy battle getting the lion protection bill through the legislature. You should know there is a severe penalty for killing a lion now."

"Thanks, Mrs. Byrd," Harry said.

But she wouldn't let up no matter how quietly he responded.

"So if you have any ideas of killing the lion, you should think twice."

"Ma'am, we're talking different languages. I've never even wanted to kill a lion since I homesteaded this ridge. But if he comes against me, I'll knock him down. It's that simple."

"Times have changed, Mr. McAlister," she said crisply. "You cannot kill a lion today without a permit and you must have positive evidence that the lion is a dangerous depredator."

"Thanks again, Mrs. Byrd." Harry resisted the temptation to mouth off about his way of life as compared to the wife of an insurance executive in her aluminum, black windowed, all electric, air conditioned domicile perched on a hill above the sea, an eyesore to anyone who'd lived on the coast or appreciated that slope before it was used as a cute foundation for a home away from another home in Palm Springs and another in Taos.

He went back to filling the woodbox with dry oak logs, thinking he'd ought to take the damned phone out.

He looked at the gray sky before going inside. It would rain again before morning.

Greta had worked extra hard on dinner. He wondered at the great spread for just the two of them. A leg of lamb, rare and juicy, peas and carrots, baked yams, red cole slaw, and a cherry pie.

She put a cold bottle of champagne before him, and two old hollow stemmed champagne glasses.

"What the heck is the occasion?" he laughed. "Should I have put on my Sunday suit?"

"You're the strangest man in the world," she teased. "Don't you know it's New Year's Eve?"

"No. To tell the truth, I didn't. If I can remember our anniversary, I'm doing pretty good."

After dinner he read the paper and a few pages of John Muir while Greta carded and spun the best wool from last summer's clip.

He watched her patient hands and her serene expression and thought. *We're too old-fashioned. We're turned backward in time, out of key, out of society. Still, we wanted to be self-sufficient and independent.*

The print blurred under his eyes and he yawned. "Time for me to go to bed. I'm not going to wait to hear Auld Lang Syne."

He stripped and boarded the rocking waterbed. He liked the bed because it eased the pain in his hips, and he liked to sleep nude because it felt natural to him.

He was nearly asleep by the time Greta turned off the lights and joined him, but some sense of crisis bothered him, keeping him from oblivion. As he drifted along, he was brusquely awakened by the distinctive blatting of anxious sheep. Warm, muzzy, he dreaded going out into the wet, cold night. He grabbed a flashlight and, completely naked, charged out of the house and up the rise toward the sheep pen.

He wasn't aware of the cold and wet. His single goal was to reach the sheep and scare off whatever waited. He'd not brought a gun.

At the pen he aimed his flashlight into the darkness. Immediately two phosphorescent globes appeared like moons. He couldn't comprehend the steadiness, the power, the heavy easiness, the mass of cat staring back at him. She seemed enormous, pale silver in this light, smooth as moth wings, uncaring, unhurrying, feminine, a vital force flowing before his eyes. He had no sense of fear; his whole education certified that the mountain lion never attacked man.

He knew without thinking that she was female.

And he hated her. In one part of his mind he raged and insulted her on behalf of his dogs and his home.

She stared at him, and in a few moments gathered herself and leaped lightly to clear the fence, but, blinded by his light, she hit the six-foot-high mesh and, easily as a ballet dancer, turned in midair and glided back to the ground facing him again. She was not afraid of being caught, nor in any panic or frenzy. Low to the ground she flowed toward him.

And naked in the cold wet, Harry waited and stared and absorbed, trying to feel every motion and nuance, trying to intuit every sense of an animal he had never seen before in such a lonely and open way and never would again. A cresting point of his life, this meeting.

He had spent his working years to come in balance with the beast, a closeness, a harmony, not sharing, but fixing a position of mutual proximity and possibly wonder; certainly he was in wonder at himself and the night and the cat approaching him like a silvery roll of mist with luminous eyes fixed on his own.

He stood silent until she came within one easy jump, and without thinking he made a snarling sound in the back of his throat.

Turning she drifted down behind a patch of brush, and Harry ran back to the house, knowing already how late it was to load a rifle.

When he returned, the pen was empty except for two dead yearlings lying side by side like sleeping sisters, both their necks broken. The remainder of the flock huddled in a mass against the far fence, terrified and mindless.

And Harry thought of the cat, her round, smooth head with its wine-cup ears cocked up, hearing his breathing, his heart pounding, the imitation cat snarl: it was all gone.

If he had turned first to run, she'd have killed him in less than a second. Not because he was an enemy, but because he was hot-blooded, naked and running, a valid target for a cat already high on killing.

He'd been too enthralled by the vision itself to race from it. Her beauty and grace had in fact saved his life.

But by then they were locked together in a more profound engagement.

Despite all the temporizing and arguments for 'balance' there was no way to avoid the geometry of life and death. The sheep did not deserve to die. They were not even used for food. The cat simply enjoyed killing the terrified animals.

And that cat must be killed.

Greta joined him at the pen, helped him examine the rest of the sheep. One old ewe had been raked across the back, a flap of wooly hide hanging to the ground. Harry, by Greta's flashlight, cut the skin off cleanly and wiped a gob of salve across the raw haunch to discourage flies. The rest were unharmed.

"Smart lion. She kills my dogs first, then takes over. I didn't think she'd come in so close."

"What shall we do with the dead ones?"

"Bait."

Gray light shone through the mist, and they went back to the house to dress and start another country day.

Harry spent the morning in his woodshop, building a redwood slab table for a lady in Carmel who could afford his exacting craft. He had started with the tree itself, an old fallen giant in the canyon. He'd sawed the slabs with his chainsaw and hired a strong young man to help him carry them out of the canyon to his shop. A month later the slabs were legs and top, mortised and doweled in perfect congruence and, even rough sanded and unfinished, he could see the symmetry of sculpture and purpose in the heavy table.

In the afternoon he rummaged through the loft of the barn until he found five lion traps he'd salvaged years before, not knowing then why he should bother to carry them home. Thirty years they'd been waiting, and he'd never planned or even conceded that they would ever be used. Yet, why had he kept them?

The sheep grazed restlessly in the front pasture. Mac's bell rang as he moved. He was supposed to be the strong one, the defender, but he was no more than a mouse to the lion.

Do we all strut our pride and toss our heads threateningly for any purpose, and isn't there always a giant coming from the darkness?

A light drizzle fell and the sun never came through. A gray, depressing day that hung like mold on Harry's thoughts. He didn't want to kill the lion. He didn't even want to see her again, though the vision was such a wonder.

Towards evening he locked the sheep in their little house where they were crowded and blatted miserably, but they were safe. When they were secure, he took the steel traps into the pen where the dead lambs lay, soggy, inert, swelling.

The traps were not meant to be staked down. Instead a small steel anchor hung on each chain. The lion was to be caught, given a run until one of the hooks caught a piece of brush, then, hung up like a fish on a line, she would fight the pliable brush until the executioner arrived.

He dug shallow holes around the carcasses, and set the double-springed traps in them so that their big jaws and the quick-falling pan were level with the ground. He concealed each pan with a square of denim and sprinkled fine earth over each one until only the unobstructed steel jaws like five open sharks' mouths could be seen in the dirt around the dead sheep.

He took a wad of dead weeds and wiped the area clean of his own marks, and he laid an old redwood fencepost on an angle to direct the lion's path. Stepping back, the scene became perfectly natural, two dead lambs weathering into the earth.

He sighed bitterly, and returned to the house as the darkness of January closed down over the soggy ridge.

After supper he oiled his best hiking boots, and selected from the dusty rack of rifles the .44 magnum with its extra wide scope. The blunt cartridges were dull with age, but he figured they'd still fire. He'd bought the .44 years before to hunt nocturnal feeding wild boar that were ravaging his pastures. The heavy 235 grain bullet wasn't easily deflected by brush, and the wide scope required little light to sight in the target.

"Why don't you stake down those traps and you won't have to track the lion," Greta asked worriedly.

"Those traps will pull off with a hard jerk. Better let her wear herself out pulling on a branch."

"But suppose she gets into high brush?"

"I guess I'll go after her then." He turned out the light.

After unremembered tortured nightmares, Harry was glad to feel the dawn, and to dress in darkness.

The decision. The fading night cool and wet.

His wife slumbered in the warm waterbed. The canyon hawks slept in the top of their redwood. Nothing hunted or fled in the pale darkness. Even the roosters had not yet sensed the stormy, purple dawn. Point Sur's light turned, the Rock was in darkness.

To the east now a faint copper luster defined San Martin Top, Cone Peak, Marble Peak, Pico Blanco, real lion country.

Outside, Harry quietly jacked a blunt cartridge into the chamber of the .44. He aimed the scope at a fencepost. It was clean and clear. His hands were cold but he could squeeze a trigger.

He hoped the cat would be right there, caught and snagged up next to the dead ewe lambs. He even expected her to be there.

There was light enough now to see a California Thrasher tip off a point of mesquite to grab a bug.

He forgot time as he slowly walked up the slope, and the world slept while the great cat and Harry entered their dream.

He passed through the gate and, a step at a time, approached the trapset. The dead lambs were undisturbed, moldering away like composted leaves, but the traps were sprung, the ground clawed out in great swaths. Harry took his time and studied the scene.

Four traps were tossed and scattered. That meant the lioness had taken one with her. Hell, she could have it on her tail, she could throw it, there was no way of knowing. He remembered the vision, the huge nonchalant silvery force flowing toward him.

Remember it all, Harry, every detail, it's your life and her life, and in truth it is the essential moment.

He backed off. The smart move would be for the lion to go through the open pastures to keep the trap from fouling in the brush. Given enough time and distance, she could work out of the trap.

He looked for tracks, sign, any disturbance in the rain-rinsed morning.

A pleat in the short grass marked where the anchor had ploughed a heading across the hill straight for Point Sur.

The anchor made a dotted line clear across the short pasture, but the grass roots wouldn't hold the trap. At the fence, the homestead changed to wilderness.

He'd never tracked a lion before, and in heavy brush the

lion had a chance to kill her hunter. He tried to allow for the new odds.

Slow, Harry, go slow. She can be hidden anywhere now, waiting. This hillside was covered with a tall mat of lupine, deep enough and thick enough to hide a whole pride of lions.

Harry felt skewered on his own past. The sheep were his sheep, the dogs his dogs. The land was in every sense his land. And the lion, therefore goddamn, was *his* lion.

A bank of ivory-yellow layered the eastern horizon now. At last the spooky shadows were gone.

He worked through the brush slowly, heart sputtering like a percolator. No sign. She'd lost him.

He cut around a cliff and crossed at the head of a rocky gulch. He tried to stay above. He didn't relish being below the cat.

He bulled down through head-high brush alongside the gulch. There had to be some sign of disturbance there or she had cast the trap in a bush and was either waiting or long gone in huge invisible jumps.

What would one trap mean to such a grand, insolent beast?

On the pass down the hill he missed the sign. He moved on west about twenty feet and worked up again, doing what he least liked. Uphill she had the advantage.

Halfway up the slope he saw a broken branch by a short mark freshly scratched in the ground.

OK, Harry, you're on her. How old is it? Hours or minutes? Was she caught early last night or early this morning? No way of knowing.

Her trail could run for miles.

Nothing for it but to track slowly along the course of the crushed brush. The lupine stood higher than his head. A helicopter couldn't have found him or the cat in that velvety green tangle.

He could see no farther than he could step, and he carried the cocked .44 with his thumb on the safety.

He moved carefully, one step at a time, trying to be soundless, trying to be measured and honest and patient.

A whole bush broken and torn to pieces. She must have snagged up and fought a long time to clear the hook. The patch of lupine looked like bulls had battled on it.

He watched for birds flying and he listened for the tiniest signals.

We are coming together, lion.

He held back a moment and heard a branch sigh. His eyes snapped but it was only a bent branch trying to return to position. Yet that would mean she'd just recently bent it. How long? A minute, five minutes? One step, fifty steps? He tried to smell her, but she had the breeze with her.

He stepped along, carefully, gently, totally alert, trailing a big lioness with maybe a dinky trap hung on her paw.

He didn't hear her, never smelled her. Suddenly he simply *knew* she was there three or four steps ahead. He searched the bland brush and quietly settled to one knee close to the ground where he could see beneath the thick foliage.

Behind the slender trunks of brush was a swatch of living brownness.

Easy. Easy. Sort it all out, Harry. Don't crowd her.

He waited, holding on one aching knee, the rifle close to sighting, safety off, but first he had to identify the animal, then parts of it. Unlikely, but still it was the color of autumn coated deer.

A movement. A close, tense ear turning behind the brush stems. That was her head. He waited. Slowly the head turned. No question now, he could see the black nose, whiskers, an eye.

Harry wouldn't be hurried.

Slowly her round, clean face turned toward him and he saw her jaws and her two majestic golden eyes gazing at him just above ground level through the twisted trunks.

Not anger. Not sorrow. A perfectly dignified acceptance.

He raised the short rifle to his shoulder and set the eyes on either side of the post in the scope, paused the most brief of moments to think, "Done," and squeezed the trigger.

In the scope he could see the pink hole perfectly placed,

slightly high and between the eyes. The head settled solidly to the ground.

He waited. Who knows what such a wild beast might do in dying?

He stood and worked through the brush. Her forelegs were huge, thick as baseball bats.

He opened the hind legs and saw the sex, and that her small dugs were dry. The tail flopped like a furry club. She would weigh 130 pounds.

The trap, snagged in the brush, held two toes on her right front paw. She was perfectly fit, there was no sign of sickness. There were no scars, ticks, fleas, no nothing. She was a prime lioness gone off course.

He thought a moment if he wanted the pelt, and he quickly decided the lion should return to the earth where she was and as she was. He took the trap from her foot and looked west out over the long sea, and silently prayed, *God of the Wilderness, let this animal's spirit soar like wind and let it be sustained.*

Moving back uphill he found he was near an overgrown jeep track, and took that way home. It was easy going though his heart was heavy with a sense of loss.

He'd hardly had a cup of coffee and told the story of the hunt to Greta than a call came from Mrs. Byrd.

"Yes, ma'am." Harry felt tired, an easing off of tension.

"About your lion problem . . . ," crisp and to the point.

"The lion is dead," Harry said, thinking she had no possible way of comprehending his complex remorse.

"You killed it?" Mrs. Byrd's voice had a new edge to it.

"Ma'am, I couldn't wait," he said, thinking it was all said, explained and ended.

Harry was just finishing breakfast when the green sedan with the blue shield logo on the door drove in.

Two game wardens dressed in green, each carrying a holstered .357 magnum pistol, stepped out, and introduced themselves.

"About the lion . . .?"

"I left her lay."

"Can you direct us there?"

"No, but I can guide you," Harry said. "It's in heavy brush."

They followed him down the jeep road.

"I don't see what all the fuss is about," Harry said. "She was a fine animal, but she was crazy to come at me three times."

"Mrs. Byrd carries a lot of clout," the younger warden murmured.

Nothing had changed. A blue bottle fly hovered over the head wound.

"You understand your right not to incriminate yourself?" the older warden asked, turning away from the lion.

Harry had the feeling that here on this brushy headland looking out over the enormous sea that he was somehow involved in a world of insects, a flea circus.

"I'm not ashamed that I killed that lion because she killed my dogs and my sheep and she would have killed me."

"That's not the point, Mr. McAlister," the older said. I have to give you a ticket."

"OK, write it out." Harry's anger tightened his speech. "I want to go home and get to work so I can pay my taxes."

"It's just our job, Mr. McAlister," the young man offered sympathetically.

Harry took the ticket and left them to figure out how to carry the carcass out for the Departmental biopsy.

All morning he split wood to work off his anger and by lunchtime he had himself steadied down.

"Them folks are dead wrong," he told Greta. "All of them. I didn't choose that lion. She chose me, and we had kind of a basic connection, like a religious ritual. I don't expect anybody but me and the lion could know what I'm talking about though."

"I think I understand some of it, Harry, but the judge won't."

"Well, I ain't goin' to lie for some stupid goddamned politician."

"Easy, Harry, don't get upset again. We'll see it through okey dokey."

A week later, Harry, in his best suit, stood before the Judge. He hadn't thought it necessary to hire a lawyer. The court-room was half filled with idle spectators and a bored game warden.

"How do you plead?"

"Judge, I killed that cat without a permit but there was reasons for it. I mean we live back up in the hills and when something comes out of nature at you, you can't wait for papers."

"Times are changing," the blue-jowled Judge frowned. "Old timers down your way are going to have to learn that the law means what it says. I think most people want the lions protected and abide by the law. I don't see why you should be an exception."

Harry's bony shoulders snapped back. "Judge, your Honor, ain't there such a thing as self-defense?"

"That's the Fish and Game Department's job. Now I'm only going to fine you $500 because it's your first offense. Next case."

"Just a second, Judge, your Honor," Harry said, feeling wholly violated in this mired process, "I have to work awful hard to save up $500."

"Mr. McAlister, your fine is $500 or ten days in jail. Next case." The Judge dismissed him with curt indifference.

Harry didn't move. He turned to face Greta across the agitated courtroom and called, "You think you can handle the ranch for ten days, girl?"

She stood, anxious and near tears. "I guess so, Harry, if that's what you want."

Harry turned back and said, "I'm ready to do my time, Judge. I'll never pay a penny for doing what was right and just."

"You're in contempt of court," the Judge yelled, pounding his gavel.

Harry walked as straight as he could beside the Bailiff, his eyes cold and determined, his heart full of hatred.

In his mind, he was yelling insults and making fantastic

speeches on the rights of natural man in a free democratic society, but his lips were tight and he said nothing.

Once in the waiting room, the Bailiff smiled and said, "You won't give me no trouble now, will you? I don't want to put the cuffs on."

"I said I'd do my time. I'm not a violent man."

"Well, you sure scared the shit out of the Judge," the Deputy chuckled. "He never seen one like you before."

At noon Harry, along with half a dozen other prisoners were hauled in a van to the old jail in Salinas where he was booked and given a clean change of denims.

He was routinely assigned to work in the jail kitchen, and given a cell which already held one prisoner, a bored, heavy-boned man whose shoulders were habitually slumped down, and whose skin was jailhouse pearl.

"Howdy, my name's Harry."

"They call me Horse. You bring any goodies in the keister?"

"I don't know what you mean," Harry said, aware that everyone in the silent cellblock was listening.

"I mean like a few balloons of dope up your asshole." The heavy man's sarcasm brought a few laughs from the line of cells.

"I'm sorry," Harry said, "I don't know the lingo, and I don't use dope."

"You don't know nothing and you don't do nothing." The cellmate's eyes were opaque blurs, seeing nothing. "Maybe you can screw. I bet when I bend you over, you'll be pretty good."

The laughter now was tentative and Harry felt lost in another strange ritual that had to be worked out as carefully as a horseshoe game or a lion kill.

"I want to tell you something, Mr. Horse." Harry moved lightly toward his antagonist. "I may just look like a popcorn fart to you." Harry grabbed the man's right forearm in his big hand and squeezed. Horse stood transfixed by the high voltage of Harry's fusing blue eyes. "But leave me be, boy. You come at me, I'll beat you like a yeller dog." Harry's hand buried deeper in the flabby flesh.

"OK, Pop, OK. It's cool," Horse murmured, staring at his blue hand.

"Hey!" a voice came from down the row, "you know old Pops stood up to the Judge? Man, he's heavy!"

"I believe it." Horse was near tears now but Harry added more pressure, his hand like a noose steadily constricting on the other's fat forearm.

"Yeah, and he killed a goddamned lion, too, and he told the goddamned wardens to go piss up a rope!"

"Please," Horse sighed, "I'm sorry."

Harry held on. "I want this all wide open. I am my own man."

Horse slowly kneeled and bowed his head in misery. "Yes, sir, Mr. Harry, please, sir, I dig you, and I'd like to be friends."

"Get up." Harry opened his hand, revealing a girdle of compressed flesh. "I'm done."

"Right on, Pops," someone yelled. "Welcome to the County Rehabilitation and Human Resources Center!"

"Thanks." Harry felt suddenly weary and choked full of sorrow. He crawled up to his bunk, and said, "I just want to do the right thing. I'm not going to pace up and down like a caged wolf and I'm not going to kiss anybody's ass. I'm going to do my time and earn my own freedom."

"Don't worry, Pops," Horse said, "go to sleep. I'll call you for supper."

Ten days later, Greta met him in the office and after he had redeemed his wallet, walked beside him to the parking lot where a group of trustees with broad brooms swept the asphalt.

"So long, Lionman," a skinny kid with drooping mustache called.

Harry waved. "Be good, Stoner."

"Shall I drive?" Greta asked.

"I am tired," Harry nodded.

Driving slowly down the scenic highway, she asked once, "You all right, Harry?"

"A zoo is full of ruined animals everybody sees," Harry

spoke carefully, "but a jail is full of ruined human beings that nobody sees. I'll never be all right again."

As they passed along the grand ridges and skirted spectacular cliffs and crossed bridges high over sudsing surf, Harry dozed, and in his sleep Greta heard him whimper and cry and saw his mouth twitch in torment. She felt like stopping the truck and kissing the hidden pain away.

When she turned off the highway onto their own rocky road, the bumps and stiff springs shook him awake.

"Good to be back," he said, sitting up straight.

4.

Green Thumb

WILD WINDS TURNED against the ridgetop homestead in that mad month of March, the westerly beating cold and crazy off its white whipped sea, the southerly coming on warm and deceiving, but always bringing a week of solid driven rain to box the compass.

The worst month to make decisions, Greta thought, wind gibbering around the eaves, mad March, mad hatter, mad as a March hare, hare-brained . . .

Still, you had to do your best, March mad or August wise.

The doctor's letter lacked his cloudy bedside manner, but it fulfilled precise clarity: $25,000, to be perfectly precise, to fix Harry's hips, a special case.

She smiled at herself as the headline crossed her mind:

A Special Case
LITTLE OLD RANCHLADY STICKS UP BANK

"Come on, Gret," she tried to dominate the day. "Get your ass in gear and quit thinking."

She cinched a scarf around her ears and braided coils of faded red hair and made herself walk out into the shrill maelstrom, her knobby knees slightly bowed against the wind-

67

blown dress, her ankles in cotton hose thick and stiff.

Damn the rich Doctors, greedy devils.

Stung blue eyes leaking into the eroded waterways of her country face, she looked westward over the ever changing panorama that dropped off the steep ridge in staggered steps of gray green brush and brown swaths of timber to the tabled alfalfa fields, ending the continent. There, like a stranded bull walrus, stood that venerable seastack named Point Sur. Layers of blustering surf racked and lifted against the bastion, obscuring its lofty lighthouse with fuming scud, ever clawing at the savaged coastline.

But even on this most unpleasant day, to her, the high homestead remained purely beautiful and self sufficient. Give Harry credit for patiently searching it out thirty years ago. Give the land credit and sun and creek that never admitted drought, but Harry had the dream and made it real.

And even if the three big sons were gone to Australia building their dream sailboat, Julia married to a traveling geologist, and Penny was off God knows where, it seemed to Greta in that bitter keening moment that no one could have dreamed better and done better, and no one deserved a new set of hip sockets more than the man who had gone without them too long.

Across the pasture she saw her tall, big shouldered husband working with the colt, the same colt that had playfully butted him a month ago and sent him to the X-rays where they read why he'd been so gimpy lately.

"Lunch, Harry!" she called against the wind. And to a drippy-nosed young man scattering chicken litter over the shaggy brown garden plot, she called, "Come, Eric, lunchtime!"

Shame to lose a good helper like Eric. He worked for so little and hardly anyone would hire him.

Keep him, she thought bleakly. We're too old and too late to save pennies against twenty-five thousand dollars.

Both big men joined her at the harvest table and hungrily spooned up shinbone soup and buttered hot fresh bread. With rumpled hair the color of winter willows, Harry was spare to the point of emaciation, and the marks in his face underscored forgotten accidents and cutting winds. Eric was heavier, his long blonde hair bleached from surfing, his bright eyes tucked back behind thick-lensed glasses, his toothy smile vague.

Harry was a worker, she thought. Always was, always will be till he can't crawl. But affable Eric was like a lost flower child to her. He always seemed short a piece of furniture in the parlor of his mind, but he was honest as a looking glass with her.

"Sonofabitch," Harry smiled, "that's a good colt. He's got more smarts than half the people I know."

"If you was to sell him, Harry," Greta tried to keep her tone free and easy, "just if, but if you was to sell him, what would he bring?"

"Maybe I could swap him for a second hand pick-up truck," Harry chuckled.

"Awright!" Eric guffawed, big mandibular teeth gleaming, and Greta wondered if the young man was really sane, but then she was aware that his eyes were steady behind those thick lenses, and studying her. "You needing money?" he asked.

Suddenly she felt Harry's eyes on her, too, and she dropped her spoon.

"No, we're okey dokey," she made a smile, "I'm not selling anything."

"Lady, remember you were going to make a fortune selling avocados. And after that failed, you spent five hundred bucks on magazine ads trying to sell Apple Pie Ridge bay leaves!"

"Far out!" Eric laughed.

"God knows there are enough bay trees growing in these hills to supply the world," Greta said. "It was a fine idea, except people won't buy bay leaves by mail."

"One thing you can bet on, Eric," Harry was still teasing, "I wouldn't trade Greta for a spotted pig, but she will never make a nickel cash money out of anything."

She blushed and felt a terrible sinking despair as Harry took his bowl into the kitchen, slipped on his windbreaker, and, still chuckling, hobbled outside.

"Something on your mind, Gret?" Eric asked as she washed the dishes.

"You mustn't tell," she whispered, "they want twenty-five thousand dollars for Harry's operation."

"Ah, so!" Eric started playing Charlie Chan. "Lady need much money. Maybe number one boy has ways."

He looked at her with those distant searching eyes that belied his goofy prognathic smile. She almost panicked. "What on earth, Eric?"

"The selling price of good dope is outrageous, lady. Twenty-five plants and Harry has new hips. Guaranteed."

"I been thinking of sticking up a bank."

"No need. Good gardener grows green grass. Number one boy sells same. Gardener gets big bucks, number one boy gets smoking."

She knew it was wrong to talk with him. He was Satan selling apples. He would sell anything. Or buy anything. But the greedy devils, what about them? She clenched her jaw and didn't answer.

"So be it." He started to turn away.

Mad March, she thought, well why not at least talk?

"Wait a second. Growing and selling marijuana is illegal and immoral and about everything else I can think of."

"And you're president of the Big Sur Whist Club."

"That stuff poisons your mind, Eric."

"I love it," he grinned. "Now acid I don't do anymore. And I don't do angel dust no more, lost too many brain cells on those trips, but lady, grass is beautiful!"

"You might be going to school and making something of yourself," she said, not righteously but a little sadly as if something had been lost, never to be recovered.

"And be a success! I seen the successes. You and Harry I call successes. No power trip, just putting it all together like land, weather, and work."

Greta put the dishes in the drainer and hoped that maybe if she fainted or if she made the sign of the cross, the tempter might go away. "Eric, I'm against drugs in any way, shape or form."

"Harry's beautiful moonshine? Wow! You know alcohol is

the most abused drug in the country."

She had no answer. She knew the statistics.

"It's your land, your money, your need," he smiled all big teeth, "I'm just suggesting an alternative."

"Let's go chop berryvine." She clenched her jaw again as if to ward off the evil apple salesman grinning at her, but the hateful image of white coated surgeons in their mansions, the greedy devils, easily overrode the simple vision of mellow Eric.

"So be it," Eric said.

In spite of the foul wind, a couple of hours' digging out wild blackberry roots with a mattock cleared her head, sent the blood to flowing, loosened her joints, and the wind burned her cheeks apple red.

That evening as Harry braided a rawhide riata by the fire and she worked on the accounts, she looked up suddenly and asked, "Whatever happened to Billy McDougall?"

"That doper kid?" Harry grumbled. "Well, he had a smart lawyer."

"I was trying to remember what he did?"

"He was arrested for growing pot," Harry snorted. "Somehow he never went to trial though. Sonsabitching crooks on both ends. Them dope people are ruining this whole country."

"Maybe it's like alcohol, Harry. Moonshine and free enterprise."

"Hell, no," he yanked at a rawhide thong. "Them people are all on welfare, all stoned out of their minds, and living at the public trough."

Next morning, working in the orchard with Eric, she repeated Harry's words with a sense of betrayal, but also with a sense of her own driving necessity. *They're all on welfare, stoned out of their minds, and living at the public trough.*

Eric made his goofy Oriental laugh. "Me? Number one boy no take welfare. Honest dope farmers no live on welfare. Honest dope farmers good for business."

She remembered half a dozen self-sufficient families who lived the basic homestead life without any visible income. They were simple younger people who came to her for advice on what to plant and when, and to ask Harry which animal did best in this area. They never stayed for dinner.

"Ah bosh," she said aloud, angered that her mind kept running after the money like a mouse after a bait of cheese. "How could we hide it from Harry?"

"Not just Harry. Everybody. Narcs, deputies, Forest Service, neighbors, rip-offs, and also Harry."

"You have it all figured out right now, don't you? Show me."

"Ready thyself then," he said, straight-faced and firm-jawed, using a line from his favorite comic book. "We go."

Always playing it silly, she thought, as he led the way over the rim of the ridge through thick coyote brush and poison oak. She glimpsed the river winding alongside the highway down in the valley, the village resort, and the helter skelter developments across on the opposite ridge. Eric went slowly, breaking the path for her.

Realizing that people might see her from the valley or from that ridge, she tried to be small, if not invisible, and she kept behind the tallest brush.

"We'll dig a little trail across here before summer." Eric stopped to wipe the sweat from his face.

Still keeping a steady fix on his destination, he broke down a tangle of brush and struggled on. She followed, her skirt snagged by thorns, her boots tangled by bindervine.

He stopped again at the base of a cliff, broken and eroded into heavy granite faces. "Let it be here." He smiled grandly, happy to disclose his dream. "Lots of sun, and the heat in these rocks all night is a bonus."

She knelt to dig a handful of topsoil, sifting it between her fingers, and tasting a bit of the dust. "It's good dirt" she decided. "Never worked a day in its life."

"We spot our plants at random, as close to the rockface as we can."

But looking down at the valley floor full of traffic and business, where old folks played croquet and the gas station pumped gas, and newlyweds strolled along the river, she instinctively ducked.

"Fear not," he laughed. "That's almost half a mile down there."

"Twenty-five plants along here?" she whispered.

"Double, allowing for half males, makes fifty. Big patch till the males are pulled."

"Can you tell the difference between the males and females?"

"I know sinsemilla from the S to the A." No longer a foolish clown, Eric was on his own ground now and proud of it.

"How high do they grow?"

"Fourteen feet maybe."

"Water?"

"I tap into the irrigation line on the hill."

"Suppose we're caught?" she finally choked the awful fear out into the open.

"You just say, that no good hippie sonofabitch Eric, I knew I shouldn't have ever trusted him!"

"Just sell you out? I don't do things like that."

"It's like a game. The cool ones know the rules. You and I know you're not selling me out, you're just making a cover for your straight lifestyle, and the law won't waste its time on my case."

"And I'm just a sweet trusting lady victimized by a rotten no-good surfer." She laughed, all the lines in her face moving the right way for a change.

"Awwww-right!"

"Harry knows every breeze, every twig that falls on this ranch," she cautioned.

"He'll know something, but not exactly what. He'll think you're two-timing him, he'll think you're going wacko, but he'll never guess you're growing dope."

"Who markets the crop?"

"Yours truly."

"And how much is there?"

"Every plant does maybe a pound say. Depending on a lot of things. Bugs, weather, rats, deer, do-gooders, thieves."

"Not up here."

"Come October, you'll be having nightmares about cops and surveyors and Forest Service inspectors, or a jerk looking for his dog."

"Mercy," she sighed, "When do we start?"

"Tomorrow. I've got some real neat Oaxacan seed and some primo Columbian Gold."

"Are they a pretty, happy plant?"

"I can't believe you!" Eric's piano key teeth shone in a wondrous smile.

Next morning after starting the coffee, she went out onto the deck to watch the sunrise, the brandy-colored light expanding against the pinks and blues on the eastern ridge, until the sun itself lifted in a fire of rosy warmth, and standing there shivering a bit in her robe, she made a little morning prayer: "Dear God, let me win."

"Anything special on the hook today?" Harry asked, kneading his hip before sitting down to his breakfast.

"Nothing much." She tried to keep her voice steady and casual.

"You catching cold?" he looked at her.

"Not me!" Her voice cracked and she laughed at herself.

"You don't look right. Better you pot plants all day."

She knew her face had turned pale. She coughed nervously and hurried to wash the dishes.

"Take some Vitamin C," Harry said on his way out.

She met Eric in the greenhouse that smelled of old molds, and wetness and sweet petunia blossoms and carnations. It was one of her favorite places on the ranch. She grew the tomato and pepper seedlings here and started begonias and ferns and cut flowers for the table, and she'd never even dreamed of growing Cannabis Sativa.

On the potting table, Eric dumped a small plastic bag of hardshelled gray green seeds.

"They're like milo maize," she said, touching them with her fingernail, "bigger than cabbage or kale."

"They're not that kind of plant. They're a hemp weed. We put them in a jar of water. Those that float are sterile. Those that sink may germinate."

In a few days when the wet seeds started to crack, Eric showed her how to tweeze each seed and plant its pointed head upright in a peat pot. "Just keep them wet, but not flooded," he said.

"Greta, are you in there?" Harry called from the upper path. "Telephone!"

Her heart stopped. "Okey dokey, Harry. Right there!" she croaked valiantly as Eric deftly slipped a newspaper over the pots where the seeds lay quietly germinating, meeting the earth for their big chance.

Harry came in the door. "I don't think it's anything. Just somebody wanting to know about local herbs."

"You're the expert." Eric said.

Greta felt a bit dizzy. Never in all their years together had she ever held anything back from her husband.

"I could use a hand stretching fence today," Harry said.

"So be it." Eric's eyes never faltered behind the thick lenses. "We go."

Lovely early May, a time of a few showers and a lot of sun came like honey to the ridge, and Greta mothered fifty plants that flourished under the fluorescent grow-lights in the greenhouse. She had trouble hiding them all. They'd been repotted into larger containers and each branching plant was over a foot high, all healthy, strong, and nitrogen green. Yet the ladies of the community often visited, and Harry sometimes came down for one reason or another, so that she started locking the door, and constructed a screen around the plants just in case.

Already her energy was going into the plants, worrying about bugs, discovery, health, sex. Suppose all fifty were females!

She thought perhaps a truly loving gardener could talk them into their sex and she started calling them all girls.

And one day when Eric was inspecting the plants, explaining that the Mexicans hadn't sense enough to root out the males, therefore they could never grow the true and precious virgin sinsemilla, she interrupted, "We ought to have the site prepared."

"Always thinking," Eric grinned, and she knew then that probably the Mexicans couldn't root out the males from their fields, but neither could Eric get his plans in motion unless someone pushed him.

While he worked at tapping into the water line, she dug holes at the base of the cliff where she meant each plant to go. She terraced the rich earth and each day she carried buckets of chicken manure down the side hill on the covert path.

The plants grew rank and ungovernable in the greenhouse, demanding to be released into the environment, and with Greta pushing him on, Eric finally managed to conceal the plastic pipe all the way to the foot of the cliff.

Every night when she said her prayers she asked forgiveness for her duplicity to Harry, and for breaking the law, and then she silently asked the Lord for His help in making the money to fix Harry's hips.

Glazed-eyed and bleary, Eric studied the great redwood log and nodded. Harry looked at him. He kept on nodding, the smile fixed on his face.

Harry gritted his teeth and looked again. Still nodding.

"Damn it, Eric, you better go on back home till you can handle yourself."

Eric continued to nod as Harry's words slowly revolved through his cottonball mind.

"Hear me, Eric? This work is too dangerous for dopers. It's your own brain, you got a right to burn it, but I don't want you dropping a log on me. I hurt too much already."

"So be it." Eric carefully shaped each syllable from the slow convolutions of his distant brain, turned like a slow motion firewalker, and floated away.

Harry kicked the log in anger and instantly felt the pain go all the way into his hip. "Damn fool," he growled.

And at lunch he complained, "Dim-damn it, Greta, I can't handle that big timber by myself. I surely wish the boys would come home."

"I'll help. Or Eric will be okey dokey tomorrow."

"I don't want him. Sonsabitchin' dopers. Pot-smoking bums. I'm getting so I just get sick with hate."

"He's young yet, Harry." She turned away to hide her face.

"I got a notion for a windlass that I can build to move those logs by myself," he muttered, already preoccupied with the problem. "I think I can weld a tripod . . . ." He left the kitchen and limped out the door.

Next morning Eric arrived, sweet as candy, sunburned hair, big horsy smile and gentle clever eyes. "Morning lady, how's the old plantation?"

"Eric," she said carefully, "You been a bad boy."

"Guy gave me a pill. Best bomb I ever ate!" He laughed, "Wish I had a thousand more. I rode the waves all day."

"Harry's mad and I'm worried."

"We go." he said.

In the greenhouse, Eric fondled the bright green plants. "Kiss me baby," he touched his lips to the crown of the nearest plant.

"Suppose it's a male?" Greta teased.

"Yuk, Greta, you got a twisted mind."

"Harry goes to the soil conservation meeting today. Time we moved them out."

"So be it."

And when Harry rattled down the road in his old truck, they met like conspiratorial lovers, smiling and warm, their steps light as naughty children's.

She gently placed each plant in its hole at the cliff base, pressed good soil around the ball of roots, and gave each a drink of water fortified with Vitamin B-1 to ease the shock.

Fifty plants were too crowded, but it was the only way they could hope to end up with twenty-five producing females. Chance would decide which would be removed and give room to the others.

Over each plant she put a plastic cap to keep it warm in the first few nights of its life outside.

"Plane going over right now can spot those white caps like a robin spots a worm," she complained.

"They won't even start looking until August," Eric reassured her. "From now on, it's grow grow grow."

Summer came on like a warm blooded horse, never heavy enough to drive the people into the shade, but still yielding enough fire to bring sugar to the fruit and growth to the grass.

"Garden ain't quite so strong this year," Harry commented one evening as they watched the sun set beyond Point Sur like orange ice cream melting into the silver sea.

"Maybe a little cool this year," she said, knowing full well that she hadn't fed nor weeded the tomatoes nearly as much as usual.

"I guess," he sighed shifting his leg to accommodate the misery in his hip. "Seems like it's been hotter this year though."

"No, it's been lots colder, I said."

"Don't be so pecky," he looked at her closely. "I swear you been nervous as a chippy in church all spring."

"Maybe I worry more now. Security, old age, health."

They watched the final flash splash of golden sun into the graying sea and felt the cool shadows rising up from the redwood canyons.

"Don't worry, girl. We got a ways to go yet." He leaned over and kissed her cheek, and she nearly wept.

In some odd sense of communion, she named each plant and spoke to them all as if they were growing maidens. Every morning, as soon as she could evade Harry, she would clamber over the fence, hiking her skirt up indecently, disappear into the brush, and emerge at the cliff base garden.

"Good morning, Lois," she greeted the first in line. "Good morning, Betty Sue . . . Diana . . . Gracie . . . LaVonn . . . Gail . . . Melissa Jane . . ." checking their ground for too little or too much water, examining the branches of serrated leaves for signs of sex Eric had promised would show before August.

When the wood rats attacked, Eric scattered boxes of rat poison through the plantation. The rats hauled off the poison at night and still nipped off branches at random, carrying them away to distant nests.

"Every one of those branches will make a top worth a hundred bucks," Eric said bitterly as he examined a nearly denuded plant.

"I can set traps. That way we're sure we're catching them."

"So be it. I have to get back to helping Harry split posts before he fires me for incompetence." Eric laughed and hurried back up the trail.

Ah, poor Harry. Everyone deceiving him. But, by golly, it's for his own good, it is.

That afternoon she bought half a dozen rat traps and, sneaking over to the patch at sundown, she tied half a walnut to each tongue and set the traps all through the besieged plantation.

Next morning early, "Hello, Lois . . . Maureen . . . Belle . . ." she found she'd caught five big wood rats and a bluejay.

Discarding the thick gray bodies, she reset the traps, pleased to see that no more branches had been nipped off in the night.

In mid-August, she and Eric prowled through the rows of plants high as her head, admiring the luxurious growth, the massive trunks, when he froze like a pointer on top of a covey of quail.

"Hey," he growled, bending a top closer to his glasses. "Hey, that's a male sonofabitch! See the balls?"

He touched two tiny green buds at the base of a branch with his fingernail. "Yank the bastard!"

"Wait," she said, "that's Jessie."

"That's a faggot. Pull him out."

"But it's too soon," she pleaded. "Maybe they're just leaf buds."

"Lady, I know a pollen ball when I see it. All it has to do is pop open and the crop's wasted."

Out of patience, he grabbed Jessie's midriff and heaved the whole plant out of the ground.

"O dear," she nearly wept, "you don't have to be so rough."

Continuing on, he smiled and patted her sad sagging shoulder. "Now, look at this beautiful lady here."

He pointed out two white hairs in a leaf cluster, so small she had trouble even seeing them.

"That, my dear, is one female showing."

"Melissa Jane."

"Melissa Jane is beautiful, keep her growing and the rats and scale off and she'll make a pound and a half."

"Botanically," she said, studying the flower cluster, "it's most interesting. These hairs are really two stylar branches on each side of the female pistle."

"Good smokin', lady." Eric smiled.

"How much will a pound and a half bring?"

"A couple of grand easy, tax free."

They inspected each plant, tying ribbons on those identified as females and pulling out the males as they showed their sex. Each day the gaps in the rows increased and the ribboned maidens increased until she could count twenty sure females with eight as yet unidentified.

By August's end, the plantation was reduced to twenty-four plants, one less than she'd hoped for and still four of them were unsexed. Worried, Greta addressed them firmly, "No more fooling around, girls! This is the real thing, not any kid's game. Now I want you to do your best for me, and I'll do my best for you, because from now on it's shape up or ship out!"

But the best they could produce was two more males, bringing her total whitehaired female population down to twenty-two.

The daily routine of sneaking down and back on the trail, catching rats, chasing away animals and being ever vigilant for a latent male was drain enough on her energy, yet she still had to maintain the regular ranch routine of gardening, harvesting, and preserving. Cockerels and old hens had to be culled and killed and put away in the freezer, and there were always extra summer visitors, and yet she still kept a cool solid front, nodding at the right time and making the expected reply while knowing that she was in league with the devil, and that the devil in her case was the better choice.

The hypocrisy of playing whist with the Grange ladies every Wednesday night, exchanging gossip, recipes, weather talk, and the inevitable turning of the conversation to the influx of freak hippie dope growers became almost unbearable to her proper mind. " . . . They should jail every one of them . . . I'd geld them, by God, I would . . . Save the taxpayers . . . Send them by Jesus back to where they . . . Shave their heads . . . What do you think of that scum of the earth, Greta? . . ." And what could she say?

"Everything runs it's course," she'd reply, studying cards, nodding judiciously.

And Harry worried about her health, telling her she looked tired, that Eric wasn't helping her enough. Maybe she ought to have a checkup, slow down some, get a hired girl, take a vacation . . .

"Nothing wrong with me, Harry, don't worry, we'll make it through the harvest and then we'll take a vacation."

"I never saw you look so plumb worn out," he nagged, his own pain becoming so fierce he hated to walk anymore.

Bad enough all that, hard and worrisome, but then the spotter planes came cruising over, searching, photographing, recording, and you couldn't tell which plane was a private pilot or a sheriff. At odd times single wing planes and helicopters flew over. Some were army green, some were black and white, some bright red, white and blue.

Day by day they seemed to patrol closer and closer, until one warm September morning, working among the giant weeds she heard the thump thump thump of rotor blades beating the air.

The morning turned sick as the chopper dropped over the ridge and came at her. She shuddered and sank into the fragrant marijuana verdure.

The men seated in the airborne plexiglass dome were no more than fifty yards away, so close she thought they were watching her down in the plants, so close they could reach over and put the handcuffs on her and drag her off to jail.

She held her breath and prayed they were looking at the river, and she told herself she'd never do such a crazy thing again. The beat of the blades paced her thumping heart.

*. . . I'm going to pull them all, I am, I can't stand any more of this. It's not worth it. I don't want to be a jailbird, please. There has to be another way. I'll pull them and be gone before they can land . . . .*Terror struck into her vitals like slow lightning, numbing her every thought and response. She lay in the dirt, cowering like a whipped dog. She wanted to vomit.

The beating rotor moved slowly on, impersonally cruising over the valley toward Rupture Ridge.

Under her tender loving care, the plants grew to be giants, burgeoning like lush pine trees. Already fourteen feet tall, they dwarfed her as she fed their roots a rich tea concocted of fish emulsion and chicken manure. Each branch ended in a cluster of white threaded buds and each day they grew bigger and bowed the great branches down.

"I've seen most of the patches on the coast," Eric put both hands around the trunk of LaVonn and couldn't make his fingers meet,"but you've got 'em beat all to hell. Maybe we better hold them back. They look like a jungle from the highway."

"O no," she argued. "We grow the best we can. That's the promise we've made each other and it's too late to back out now."

Eric shook his head in wonder. "So be it, if we can get through to harvest."

If If If! She raged inside. Why so many Ifs?

In mid-September when the flower clusters at the top of each branch filled into maturity, the buds swelling and oozing hallucinogenic resins, crowding each other into huge kolas the size of billy clubs, the deputy sheriffs commenced their annual raids.

Eric had no explanation for their targets. "I'd guess they've got a pigeon planted on the coast that feeds them information because so far they've only hit the bigger patches."

"Maybe the girls really are too big," Greta worried, washing the breakfast dishes.

"No, no, lady," Eric teased. "You promised them a healthy life and we're going for it."

She dropped a plate. "I'm so far behind on my canning I'll never catch up," she said, her hands trembling as she swept up the fragments. "I even burned the bacon this morning."

How she regretted committing to the ladies. How she wished she'd never started caring for them!

The grand plants stood high against the cliff like a circus of green banners waving in the afternoon breeze, beckoning at the airplanes, 'Come, see the biggest show on earth!'

And every time she heard a siren wailing down the highway, she blanched and shook, and though she worked herself to exhaustion every day, her sleep was troubled by threatening dreams.

"What the heck is the matter with you?" Harry demanded at breakfast. "Toss and moan all night, drop the eggs, jitter-bugging all over the place. If I didn't know you so well, I'd think you was up to something. I'm going to send you to the vet."

"I guess it's some female complaint," she laughed quietly at her joke.

When she prayed for thick peasoup fog, the weather produced a heatwave. All day the sun burned like a blowtorch, driving Greta to the shade of an oak tree. Harry put a sprinkler on the roof just to cool off the house.

The heat-loving plants proliferated. At twilight she visited the plantation and thought her darlings had shot up another foot, and dear heaven, the great cliff rock was still hot to her hand and would keep them growing through the night.

The heat wave continued and the branches sagged with the weight of budding tops and syrupy resins. The weatherman cheerfully predicted another week of clear sunshine.

She was sure her excessive plantation had been seen either from the air or the valley. It was just a question of time now until the sheriff arrived and put her in the caged backseat and hauled her off to jail, and Harry would disown her.

No longer could she and Harry sit out on the deck after sundown when twilight shadows gathered up from the canyons and slowly flooded purple into the grand western sky. The plants were releasing an unmistakable perfume across the evening slopes, sending out their seductive musk to the plant world in an urgent appeal for pollen, for love, for immortality. What would happen if Harry ever smelled that evening breeze and put the puzzle together?

One little whiff of her ladies' extravagant sex was enough to send her inside the house to rattle tin pans and drop things.

She lost weight and had none to spare. Harry insisted she go in for a check up, but the doctor's response was more vitamins and a Valium prescription.

"Anything worrying you?" the doctor asked as she was leaving.

"Harry's hip joints."

"Yes," he assumed a remote manner. "He's at the stage where if they're not taken care of, he'll soon be in a wheel chair."

"Book him in for late fall," she said, angry at his flaccid determination of a human tragedy that couldn't touch his heart. "I'll have the money."

She rode home with Harry, feeling desolate, carrying a heavy world on shoulders she wasn't sure could carry the load.

He pulled into Apple Pie Village for gas, and she couldn't resist looking high up at the ranch, looking up at the granite cliff, looking up at the jungle of bright green plants waving like young pine trees in the breeze where no pine trees existed.

She shuddered and Harry looked up.

"Deer!" she croaked pointing off to the left. "Big buck."

"Funny time for bucks to be out," Harry said, and spoke to the attendant. "Fill it up, please."

The great unfertilized kolas drooped now like shaggy green clubs, bowing down the limbs of the spectacular forest, forcing Greta to tie and guy the trunks to the fractured cliff wall.

"When, O Christ, Eric, when can we harvest these things?" she begged, her weary eyes framed in dark circles.

"Hang on, lady. You see these brown hairs, coming out of the cotyledons, well they've got to be darker and bigger, and more resin has to come out and cover these buds like sugar. O you beauty!" he embraced the big plant that seemed to breathe its own heavy fragrance.

"But the cops are everywhere," she said. "Every day in the paper they're hauling away somebody's crop and sending the grower to jail."

"Wrong. No grower is going to jail. They're just harassed. Myself, I think the cops pick a ton, and bring in a pound for evidence."

"Eric, in no way can I stand being taken in and messed over. Believe me."

"Easy, sweetie. Better worry about three bad dudes in a blue van. They've got trail bikes and they're scouting the whole coast."

"You mean they're hijackers?"

"Hijackers, rustlers, thieves, whatever. They make their bread stealing crops. They know they can't be reported or busted. Just drive in, rip off the plants and drive off, and you have to stay mum."

"Eric, why didn't you tell me?"

"I told you there were heisters and cops and that September and October would be a ball."

"Yes, you did," she sighed and sniffed the heavy fragrance of a foot and a half long kola.

"When?" she shook her head wearily.

"We harvest on the full moon."

"But everyone is after us!"

"No, you just think so, unless you've been talking."

"I don't talk, Eric, but the planes, the heisters! The gas station!"

"Easy, easy, lady. Two weeks isn't so long. Like I said, anything happens you blame it on me."

"Now you're making me feel bad," she said, deeply troubled

by her guilt and her willingness to let him be the scapegoat while she hid behind an unbearable hypocrisy.

Three young men got out of the blue van and stretched their legs lazily. Greasy long hair, sunglasses, interchangeable in soiled Levis and sportshirts, but their pallid complexions marked them as street people. Mustaches, beards, long hunting knives in their belts. Hard to keep them separate except one was short and fat and jolly and did all the talking.

"Howdy ma'am." Immediately she knew the flummery of his approach. "We're just out looking for some good ground."

"We get a lot of boys dropping by that want to get back to the land." She hoped her trembling hands would look as if she had the palsy.

"Would you be knowing of any kind of garden ground with water?"

God, she thought, how stupid does he think I am?

"Well boys, we own all this. Our sons are off in Australia but it'll be their ranch when they come back."

"You folks just up here on top of the world by yourselves?" The fat talky one nodded, his eyes wandering behind the dark glasses.

"Just me and my husband and he has bad hips, can't hardly move anymore. I tell you boys, you could be doing us a big favor if you'd help pick the apples."

The other two young men strutted on stiff legs about the yard restlessly, speaking short phrases in undertones.

"That right ma'am? Well, we'd be mighty proud to help later on," Fatty beamed. "Would you mind if we was to ride our bikes on up the hill?"

"Not a bit," she declared. "You go right ahead." She paused to reflect. "Well now maybe we better clear it with the Forest Service. They're always worrying about me and Harry being up here by ourselves and the Mount Manuel Firewatch keeps an eye on us. They see some motorbikes driving on up the hill they just might send a fire truck or something. I'll give them a call if you like."

The fat one looked at the other two, waiting, until one pursed his lips in a sneer and said, "No way."

"Beg pardon?" she said.

"It's nothing ma'am. We just lookin' for a piece of land to lay our heads on, and if there ain't none around this ridge I guess we'll just have to mosy on."

"But there's apples need picking."

"We'll be back, ma'am. It's been real good talking to you."

Hard-eyed, they seemed to slink like snakes sneering into the blue van, and without a wave drove on back down the road, leaving Greta shaking and laughing and crying, because by God she had whipped them at their own game and so she wasn't just a dumb country woman after all. She was, by God, as bad as the baddest!

And each night when she watched the moon grow a bit rounder, she'd whisper, "Hurry, mister moon."

Arrests every day now, kids, old beatniks, even a candidate for sheriff, hauled to jail, their crops confiscated and gone somewhere. Stories in every newspaper now of crazy people trying to extort crops, shootouts in heists, knifings, a man killed in Santa Cruz, a gang from L.A. raiding a patch, caught by vigilante growers and beaten . . . .

"Looks like every rotten bum in this country is either raising marijuana or stealing it. I don't see how the law can allow such goings on." Harry laid the paper down, groaned quietly, and took off his shoes by the easy chair.

The plants were weighted near to breaking, their heavy tops flooding a marvelous perfume, begging and groveling on the breeze for a bit of pollen to achieve fruition, but there were no males left, no pollen, until one day as she walked through the plants, she saw on Maureen's lower branches a series of altered buds. She looked twice, alarmed, her heart pumping, because she knew well enough by now that one little touch of gold across her ladies' sex would destroy the cash crop.

Sure enough, as she examined the odd branches, they were male pollen sacs, just ready to burst open, little green balls full of the future, and yet on the other branches were female cotyledons, like giant green vulvas, opened nakedly and insisting that they were beautiful.

In desperation this plant had changed its sex. A hermaphrodite, bisexual, capable of seeding itself, as well as the rest of the patch.

Impatiently she waited for Eric to see this wonder. But he didn't regard it as a wonder, he saw it as an attack. A killer. "Pull it," he said.

"That's Maureen, she's too good to waste!"

"Too damned bad," he said, "but you've got no choice. Off the faggot lesbian sonofabitch!"

"Eric, it's a beautiful huge plant."

"All ready to have a party and ruin us. You want me to do it?"

"I don't have the heart." She walked back up the trail, her shoulders down, weighted with murder.

The moon made an oval pie for her that night. Knowing she could do nothing about it, she still fretted. Those plants needed a certain photoperiod of sunlight to reach maturity, and were tied to the moon as all other women. You might not like it but you couldn't change it.

Only twenty-one plants now. Were they big enough to make up for the losses?

"My hip says it's going to rain," Harry muttered in the morning.

"O dear. It wouldn't."

"We get a freak early storm some years."

When Eric arrived at the plantation she told him of the rain coming, confirmed by the weatherman on the radio. To her own senses all she needed was a south breeze to predict rain and there it was, bending the giants toward the north.

"So be it," he decided. "Rain washes off the resins. Better not chance it. Every other grower is behind us in maturity and they can't harvest, but we're early. Where's Harry?"

"He's hurting so much, he's staying inside."

Eric didn't hesitate, but started lopping kolas from the first plant with pruning shears. "Thank you, LaVonn . . . thank you, Melissa Jane . . . ."

"O dear," she said, carefully filling a plastic bag with the heavy sticky tops, sweeter smelling than any rose.

They traded off work, lopping, filling the bags, carrying the bags to an old sheepshed where Eric tacked the branches on rafters, until, by noon, they had a festooned shed so full of drying marijuana the ceiling was hidden.

"Now all we have to do is keep Harry out and the law and the blue van and all the strange kids going by," Eric said tiredly, "and the rats, too."

"How long now?" she sighed.

"Week or two, depending on weather."

And as he spoke, a drop of rain tapped her cheek, and she smiled and wept at the same time.

They sat at a work table in the sheepshed, each with scissors and a pile of fat kolas, and Eric showed her how to snip off the little leaves that wedged out of the sugary cotyledons, and how to leave the longest tops intact. "These big clubs are special. Movie stars pay big bucks for them."

"There's so much!"

"Don't knock it, lady."

In an hour, their fingers were caked with brown sticky resin. "Know what that is?" Eric dreamily sucked his thumb clean. "That, lady, is pure hashish."

Harry was hurting too much to do much more than feed the stock. Greta didn't want to credit his pain for the blessing of free time that was given her and Eric, but she used it to the maximum. Hours and hours they spent delicately picking out tiny leaves and snipping the brown hairs from the great thick tops, until it seemed they had manicured a mountain of the stuff. The dry and brittle sinsemilla Eric weighed into plastic bags, sucked the air out and sealed them, until there were two big boxes ready for sale, the first five pounds of finished product.

"You want to sell it now or wait for a better price?" Eric asked.

"Sell it," she said. "Sooner the better."

"So be it."

Damn it, she cursed in her mind, this comic book idiot is handling thousands of dollars of my money.

But in three days, he twitched his eyebrows, showed his mandibles, looked over his shoulder to make sure they were alone and gently laid a roll of hundred dollar bills in her hand. "Count 'em. Friend dealer says it's killer weed and only takes a hundred bucks a pound for his cut."

She'd never seen so many hundreds together, and it was such a pleasure to feel their smooth skin as she counted seventy-five bills. Somehow she couldn't believe it. An incredible event. The translation of all the summer's anxiety into this nice packet of green paper. But it was an eerie scandalous sensation, too, a kind of naughtiness she'd never known, and it was fun. She giggled. She punched Eric on the arm and looked into his stoned eyes and laughed out loud and swatted him again. "That's it, Eric. It's real!"

"Buy the man a new hip, buy a Mercedes Benz, buy a color TV, buy a night on the town. Let it be so."

"You should have some," she said.

"I take my smoking. That's all."

"Let's get to work," she said and tucked the bills into the celadon cookie jar.

They attacked another heap of dried kolas, and the next five pounds went faster, and the money came right back to her eager hand.

The pounds were going fast and she felt a sense of loss and insecurity. What would happen when they were all gone? Sure, there were all those bills in the cookie jar, but what was left? It wasn't like selling eggs or strawberries because with them there was always more coming.

In this busy time, she had unspeakable ideas that she tried to put aside. Suppose Eric was being victimized by the dealer? Suppose this beautiful crop was really worth about three thousand a pound and they were only getting half, and then, too, suppose Eric, his eyes always inscrutable, was selling it for more and holding back the extra money? She had to grit her teeth sometimes to hold back her crazy accusations.

From the last batch, Eric made a special package of the largest tops they'd saved. Each kola was a giant club nearly two feet long, and, except for the stem, all pure sugared buds. "This box goes for big bucks. Two pounds, six grand."

"It'd be nice to have a bit of a bonus," she sighed.

"And I keep five pounds of straight run for myself. That's my year's smoking. Fair?"

"More than fair, Eric." She knew how greedy and suspicious she'd become, and shamed herself.

Two days later, he laid the last roll of hundreds in her hand, and her cookie jar was stuffed with four hundred and twenty one-hundred-dollar bills, forty-two thousand dollars.

She laughed everytime she walked near it, until Harry growled at her. "I wish you'd tell me what's so funny. I could use a laugh."

"O, I guess I'm getting silly in my old age," she replied, her eyes wet. "It's just that the summer has been so long and the harvest so big, more than I ever expected."

"The squash didn't do much."

"No, but we got through it. We beat the devil," she was speaking to the Chinese porcelain jar on the shelf. "We pulled it off."

"Pulled what off?"

"All of it. Don't you see. The whole ball of wax, the whole enchilada." She giggled, silly as a school girl.

"Crazy as popcorn in a hot skillet." He shook his head and smiled.

"Really, Harry, I was checking through our health insurance," she said soberly, "and I think your operation is covered."

"Funny you never saw it before."

"It's just a small piece of fine print, but I bet you'll walk like new by Christmas."

Harry greeted Eric as he floated in the door. "This woman's flipping out, Eric, she thinks she's found me a cure."

"Aww-right!" Eric grinned wide, his eyes always hidden back there somewhere.

"When it comes to money, she's got a great imagination," Harry chuckled. "Remember how she was going to make a fortune selling organic bay leaves by mail order?"

"And spent the egg money!" Eric laughed with Harry, while Greta's face flooded crimson.

"Aw, come on, you guys," she smiled shyly. "Once in awhile I do something right."

"Right or wrong, lady," Eric rolled his eyes toward the ceiling, his face beaming like a radiant ode to joy. "You sure do it well."

5.

The Gentle Shepherd

IN THE MORNING Harry liked to feed the sheep a modest grain ration because they were pets and it suited him to be a gentle shepherd. Sometimes he fed them surplus apples off the trees in the fall, sometimes lettuce or spare roasting ears from the garden.

Usually Mac and his five ewes shouldered and butted each other to be first at his hand. But there were none that morning. Where were they?

Looking west over the front lawn to where it cracked steeply off into the Big Sur valley, Harry's vision blurred the distant irrigated fields between mountains and ocean, but instantly settled on the decayed dogtooth of Point Sur, a far fang of rock, brown and crusted with salt and shorebird lime, and surrounded by rolling, gnawing surf.

In the grand clear dewy morning he stood tall, big shouldered, and apprehensive. He sniffed the air like a wolf.

Last year, before they had taken his hips apart and put them back together again, he'd felt crippled, emasculated, and old enough to die, but now that he could roam the ranch without pain, new juices steadily mounted powerful passions in his bloodstream, exciting impatience and a fear of time and vigor passing before he was ready. He felt strong as a young bull.

Peppy, his brown feist, came trotting to say good morning. Her chin was gray, her back sagging. Good morning, you old bum. He scratched Peppy's ears, worrying.

Looking south he checked the green side of Rupture Ridge for new ulcers. When he first came here the ridge was ancient and untouched. He'd thought no one would ever build over there because it was too steep, in shade most of the day, no roads, water or power, and the ground wouldn't grow enough to feed a goat. Now he looked at bulldozed pads, raw mouthfuls ripped out of the haunch of the natural ridge, adorned with houses that looked more like machine shops.

Sometimes he could hear their stereos and bongos or their dogs barking if the breeze were southerly.

The sheep were on Peppy's mind as well as his own. Tail down, she gradually moved back to her bed under the porch.

Whoo, sheep! Whoo, sheep! Harry felt a sickness tightening in his chest, knowing something was going to hit soon, and his body was already girding up to meet the shock. Whoee sheep!, he whooped into the clear morning sky that melted into the sea at land's end.

A hawk wobbled stiffly on the morning thermal and shrieked his game starting call. Whooee!

Across the fields beyond Point Sur, the endless ocean slopped a white mop against the ragged land. Greens and brown, blues and whites, and the orange sun glistening off the shoulder of a bay colt.

No sheep came bounding like funny puff balls on pogo sticks.

He went through the gate and searched high grass and brush, picking up to a frantic helpless crazy gallop before he found them piled into the lean-to at the north corner of the pasture. The ewes were due to lamb that month.

He passed the first one, her head extended, throat ripped out, and he dragged at the hind legs of others driven head first against the wall, packed in like heavy bolsters, all lifeless.

He was muttering, cussing, nearly crying. Two of them had gashed legs and broken necks. Mac had been gutted, and three were ruptured and suffocated or dead from shock, no need to know. Such fine-boned, lovely animals, each a unique tough Scot, but they were all dead. Sometime during the night they'd been chased, cut down, driven in a frenzy against the wall.

Hard to find tracks in the grass. The cut-up dust in the shelter was confusing. It might have been a mountain lion, but there were only a lot of dog tracks.

A motley pack, some of the dogs must have been big and some small and fine.

Damn, damn, beautiful, healthy sheep, smooth slender ankles and perky little ears poking out of fleecy ruffs. Dead, they looked stupid.

He walked about, sick, searching for some worth, something redeeming in the badness, but all Harry could find were a few silky, copper colored hairs caught in a sliver of a fencepost. Irish setter, Golden retriever maybe, but he knew of none in the neighborhood.

He used the truck and, after dumping the carcasses over a downwind cliff, he washed his hands and went into the house for breakfast.

"I've been waiting half the morning," Greta spoke with perfect numbing effect.

"Something killed the sheep, the whole flock." He tossed Mac's brass bell on the table.

She cocked her head sidewise, closed her eyes, and asked for confirmation, "All of them?"

"That's what I said. It was dogs."

"Sure it wasn't another lion?"

"I killed the lion. It was dogs."

"And next month there would have been a lot of little lambs out there frolicking around. Will you butcher?"

"I dumped them".

"Why not save the wool?"

If she wanted to shear a bunch of dead sheep, she was welcome.

"Harry, don't take it so hard. You'll figure a way to start over."

He didn't want to talk. He went outside to the truck. Too

late. Too late to sell out, too late to pioneer again. Too late for another private farmstead in another country. Too late for a new family. Too damned many people, too damned many dogs, too damned many years spent accumulating excess baggage.

Too damned many people. The rural community wiped out. The rugged and often demented old-timers simply overwhelmed by numbers.

The taxes doubled, yet the land was rezoned so he couldn't cut it up for his children, couldn't build income rentals, couldn't build any structure in the touring mob's 'viewshed.'

Yet what could be worse than ranchettes, shopping centers, and artificial resorts of 'development?'

His rough dirt road switchbacked down the mountainside into the valley.

Such a grand dewy day, all blue and green. The sheep fitted so perfectly within their environment, nibbling across the verdant pastures, all such a grand harmony, damn, damn! It wasn't too much to ask, was it?

Near the bottom Harry passed through his old redwood gateposts with the weathered, carved sign overhead: APPLE PIE RANCH. Forty years ago that name was a dream. Now it was his biography.

He turned into a blacktopped driveway marked with an aluminum letter sign: DARVEY. Big old oaks along the driveway offered some privacy, but the house was young. They only put one nail in each end of the studs, the sheetrock was the thinnest, and the concrete short. He'd watched the contractor from L.A. throw the house together, saw him pull the reinforcing steel out of the foundation forms just after the building inspector left.

A big white poodle barked as he parked the truck. Cutely clipped with pompoms around his ankles and another crowning his blocky head, the poodle stood on his hindlegs and scratched at Harry's door as he pushed his way out.

"Get down, you sonofabitch," Harry said, and he pulled back.

"Hello, Harry!" Beaming smile, eyes a blur behind thick

blackframed glasses. Pendleton shirt. A pencil in his pudgy
hand signaled that Harry was interrupting screenwriter Darvey's work. "Come on in."

"No, thanks, Darvey. I'm in a hurry."

"Always in a hurry. What'll it get you? What it'll get you is a
coronary. Takes one to know one. So what can I do for you?"

Darvey was never quite all there, sort of like his house. He
was shorting on the steel in order to veneer the walls.

"Dogs killed my sheep during the night."

"Oh Christ! Harry, that's terrible! Did you see 'em?"

"No, but if the dogs are packing up and traveling that far,
things will get hurt, maybe a child."

"Well, it couldn't have been Tony. He sets his butt right
there guarding the front door all night."

"You never know about dogs. Good dogs, bad dogs, they
pack up, and they change."

"Not Tony, he's true blue."

"There's an old rule about dogs running wild."

"Sure, Harry, but that was before telephones. You ever see
Tony running on your place, don't shoot him, just give me a
call, OK?"

Darvey was sharp enough, a Hollywood competitor, smiled
a lot, knew you should humor the white haired gaffer along,
but show your teeth just enough.

With Harry, it was too much. Darvey liked his poodle, but
he liked his sheep, too.

"Have a good one, Harry," he said as Harry climbed into the
truck. He hustled back inside, holding his pencil like a scalpel,
back to heal a cancerous script in Intensive Care.

Harry sniffed the sheep smell wiped off the face of the big,
lumbering poodle. True blue Tony, probably got an A plus in
obedience school.

Another hundred yards, another driveway. This one lettered in hammered black iron: PATTIMAR. Margaret was dominant, Patti the pale invisible presence in the corner. Harry
couldn't understand lesbian sex, lesbian menstruating, lesbian
oestrus, lesbian with child, lesbian milking.

Margaret came out into the yard to quiet her two Afghans,

long-limbed, silken-haired dogs, too exotic for Big Sur brush and ticks and foxtails, but they were richly colored, supple, showy animals.

Patti stayed inside the concrete block walls but she was listening at a tall, narrow window of the sunless house.

Margaret was a blunt barrel, built about like Darvey. Butched hair, stob of a face, freshly shaved.

When Harry tried to tell her his errand, she stepped up close with a challenging hostility. He hated the waste of his errand already.

"Now look, Harry, don't bug me about my dogs, see. They're the absolute primo best, harmless like me unless they're crowded. You want to grump around, don't come grumpin' around here. We don't need it."

The two dogs danced around the yard like choreographed maple leaves, so graceful and flowing. He was sick of the duality, and he doubted his own good sense.

He tried to tell her that running wild dogs were menaces. She cocked a fist.

"You better understand that anybody hurts one of my dogs, I'll have the sheriff knocking on his door and my lawyers will be suing for every cent..." On and on.

Back in his truck again he knew he couldn't move them to take care of their pets. These people cut him down. They used their dogs as advance scouts, as weapons. They might not think so, might not even know it, but his empty pasture knew it.

The next stop was different, though still the basic bulldozed pad cut out of the hillside. The sign, made of pebbles and bottle tops, said "Harvest." The man's real name was Macy, something like that, inherited merchant money. Paid cash for the place and Welfare from then on. Harvest was tall, curly gray beard, grizzled hair wrapped in a silk kerchief. Hippie pantaloons and fancy patched shirt, love all over his stoned features. His woman was no longer a chick, and four naked kids scrambled around the yard, playing with a brown, misbegotten husky-Doberman mix. The dog looked as dilapidated and spacey as everything else in the Harvest menage. And

Harry thought it all so typical that Harvest himself was a standardized, predictable cliche.

A combination of two smart breeds, the dog was a stupid loser. He still had a wisp of wet wool between his front teeth. He grinned foolishly when the kids climbed on his back. And when Harry made his wild dog speech, Harvest, projecting a sense of sage-like profundity, answered quietly, something about everything has its time and place, and love begets love, and good old shaggy Peacepipe knows his space, man, and that's all any living thing needs, right?

"But if he forgets, reverts to being a wolf?"

"Like Dracula on moonshine, or Frankenstein—wow! Far out! Don't worry, he's cool, man. His trip is happytime—besides, wolves are great."

"I know." Harry had spent some years in Alaska, and he did know. "But not if they kill just for fun."

"Old Peacepipe though, he's mellow. I feed him a special doggie biscuit." Harvest crackled with mocking laughter, as if Harry couldn't possibly know a green brownie.

Whether he liked it or not, Harry had to talk to Amy Lou Robinson.

Her house had a peekaboo view of the ocean and the yard was full of flowering plants and shrubs, because of more sun in there than most of the lots. Even so, the sun rose an hour later and set an hour earlier than up on the ridge. There was hardly room to turn around in the parking area bulldozed out of the hillside. She'd planted ivy on the bald cut, but it didn't hide the scar.

The damned Dalmatian started yapping hysterically, running around and around the truck. Of all the average sized dogs in the world, the coach dog had to be the dumbest.

He wasn't being a watchdog, he was just making an insane racket.

"Hush, Roger, quiet now." She spoke softly to the dog as Harry tried to ignore his antics.

At the garden gate, a short, snub-nosed lady with a nice smile. Her hair, veined with silver, was done up in a bun.

"Hello, Harry," she greeted him, holding out her hand. He noticed the arthritic joints and he took it very gently. Roger leaped into the back of the truck. He sniffed around, smelled the dead sheep odor, and cowered.

"What a pleasure," she said, and asked if he'd care for some tea. Harry wanted to get the business finished, and he told her of the sheep and of his suspicions.

"I can understand a police dog or a Doberman," she spoke in a mild thoughtful tone, "but not Afghans or poodles or especially Roger, killing anything."

"You'd ought to put him on a chain, or keep him inside at night for awhile."

"But one reason we moved to Big Sur is the freedom. It hardly seems fair to treat Roger as if he still lived in New York City."

He could not dent her defense of Roger, anymore than he could dent Harvest's defense of Peacepipe. People just wouldn't believe their dogs had a basic amoral wildness.

"Eleanor look, if Roger doesn't come back some day, don't ask me about him because even if I know I won't tell you."

"I don't think I could get along without him." She was dead serious. "But I can't lock him up either."

"If you ever have to replace him, get a Labrador retriever, they're best for here."

"I don't want to think about it. It's such a lovely day." She smiled, looking at a flowering pink rhododendron, ignoring everything he'd said or tried to say.

"Goodbye, Eleanor."

"Thank you for coming, Harry." She habitually smiled, but her old eyes were lost.

No point in going further. Next would be Gary Phelps, the established on-the-road poet, next to his place was a couple named Wisenberg who manufactured serigraphs by the hundreds, and next were the nuns in the R and R retreat house, and below them was Young, the archaeologist, who had sense enough to know he didn't need a dog, then Polly Glendon, who'd lost her Pomeranian and wrote greeting cards, and then

Charlie, the heroin head, who had only a monkey on his back, and then there was Laurie Clements, the local nympho, who had a big police dog, and finally at the bottom of the road lived Sam Hodman, son of the first homesteader.

Skip the rest of them. Once of anything with Tootie was enough. Go talk to Sam.

His driveway had no sign, the house, ancient for this country, was all handsplit redwood boards and shakes. Nearby moldered an old barn of the same material. Scattered about the yard were stripped cars and tractors. He found Sam leaning into the engine of his bulldozer parked to one side.

A huge man, Sam cussed as he pounded at a bolt with a six-pound hammer.

"Hello, Harry, I hear you're screwing everything that moves nowadays," he growled over his shoulder.

"Not quite. My zipper gets stuck once in a while." Harry could laugh for the first time. "Sounds like you're havin' fun."

"Yeah, I like bustin' my knuckles. I get my jollies just muckin' in black grease." Broadchested Sam turned away from the engine and slammed the hammer down to the ground like a grimy Thor. "By God, I've made a lot of mistakes in my life, but the worst one was thinking I could out think a machine!"

"I'm the guy they send off for left-handed monkey wrenches."

"You're lucky. What can I do for you?"

Rocky, Sam's big yellow hound wandered by, too tired to bark or wag his tail.

After Harry explained about the sheep and dog tracks, Sam exploded, his big ham face beet-red. "By God, Harry, the dumbest thing I ever did in my life was subdividing the goddamned ranch. All I got to show for it is a bunch of silly assed back to nature neighbors that don't know an axe from a river. They never hike into the back country, don't fish, don't hunt, don't go museling or mushrooming, don't grow nothin'. Honest to Christ, I've got a dozen dim-witted phonies for neighbors when I could just as well have a dozen good steers grazing the hill. Now I own a hundred-thousand dollar bull-dozer that won't run! Listen here, Harry, you see my dog on your land, you bust that sonofabitch in the belly with your ought-six and I'll pay for the ammo. I don't know if he's runnin', but don't bother givin' him a murder trial, just blow him away."

That was a man Harry could understand. He wasn't intellec-tual, he wasn't merciful, but he was not a plastic, displaced neurotic either.

"Sam, I hope I don't have to."

They shook hands and Harry let him go back to fighting the machine, while he drove on back up the road to the ridge that he'd named Apple Pie. If it weren't so beautiful, the hard living that nature exacted would have been slavery.

From then on he had to keep the colt in a tight corral, and he resented it every day when he tossed hay into the pen. The colt could just as well be out eating grass on the hillsides, but he'd be no match for a dog pack.

Harry considered selling him, but a country man needed to raise something.

Raise something or move to town. Buy into one of those condominium slums tacked up all over the flood plain of the Carmel Valley. Keep a cat.

Someday he intended to ride the colt back into the Ventana Wilderness if he turned out to have good mountain feet. You didn't want a clumsy horse carrying you on cliff-hanging trails, nor one that would spook on a ridgeback. He reckoned his new hips would wear out about the same time the colt was ready.

But for now in that birthing month of April, Harry enjoyed long walks in the green hills, into the amazing wilderness. He liked to keep in time with the living system back up there: bucks and does, wild boars, how many mountain lions and coyotes feeding on them.

He studied a group of rooting wild boar on a far hillside with binoculars. A coyote lay off to one side, his nose tucked under his tail. He'd learned to travel with the herd and live off newborn piglets, the pig population ultimately decided by how often the coyote got bored by baby pork. When he pined for a juicy wood rat or bunny rabbit, he left the herd for awhile and gave the little ones their chance to grow.

The wild boar had been moving away from the highway. There'd been a time when they rooted through Harry's front yard at night, but his guard dogs chased them out, and now the dog packs were harassing them farther and farther away.

A few rifles and shotguns hung on the wall of his shop, but he hadn't hunted much since his boys grew up and went to Australia. He'd wanted them nourished by the least poisoned food available, and he'd wanted them to know that meat didn't come in a plastic skin. He hunted according to his own ideas, too. Young does in the fall, the bucks in the spring, wild boar any season. There were no game wardens or stray bystanders to worry you then.

But with the youngsters gone out on their own, he had come to the point where the blood and fleas and exhaustion from packing out a carcass wasn't worth the killing.

Now he only carried binoculars, sometimes a sketch pad.

Of course, if a deer jumped the fence into the orchard, he'd shoot him same as if he were a fox in the chicken house.

Same as with the dogs. He saw the pack once in awhile, the poodle, the Afghans, old Peacepipe, an Irish setter, but they kept to the lower elevations.

On a golden spring day, he lay back on a high green knoll and watched the clouds ghost over white and perfect as Cheviots. His mind drifted along, remembering the early wild days, remembering when he accidentally shot a boar in the nose on this knoll. Mad as hell, he'd made a run at Harry. His curved ivory tusks, fully extended, clacked like swords, but Harry hadn't thought about the danger, he'd thought he should be shooting better because his bullets weren't slowing the hog down, and then he hit him a good one, so the boar died at his feet. Harry thought about the 'moment of truth,' a gem of Hemingway's imagination. Such a moment was not for him. You killed the charging boar, otherwise he killed you. In

Harry's psyche there was no 'otherwise.'

And he didn't agree that the thrill of hunting was expressed in killing a beloved or challenging wild thing, be it pheasant or elk. A dead bird or animal or a dead person, was dead, an absolute, positive symbol of death, and there was no beauty in it, no possession, no encompassing, no cherishing. Death was death. The hunter possessed only his own death. The light gone from the radiant eye, the rainbow sheen instantly drying off fur or feather, the rot begun the moment death, not the hunter, possessed the hunted. And there was no beauty in it. Death was rot. He'd read articles by hunters who romanticized their emotional problems to the point where they would have liked to have joined Lee Harvey Oswald in the Transcendental Orgasm of the Century: Select weapon, stalk, ambuscade, perfect bullseyes under stress—*and the wild Irish light went out of Jack's eyes, the burnished glow left his hair a dusty mat, the ruddy magic heatlamp exploded, and the rot began.*

Yes, it was spring, the time of baby chicks and hillsides purple with bluebonnets, and air clear and scented with wild lilac. There on the east ridge the sun rose early, warm and pastel behind Mount Manuel, casting a mountainous shadow over the blue flint sea, meadows light and teasing with blossoms, the hills were pastures deep with juicy wild oats, busy little birds, and butterflies touching tall flowers.

The does were separating, moving toward the dangerous privacy of birth. Those were the best days. He left early, carrying lunch and binoculars, and he returned at dark to feed the colt and have supper with the wife and chitchat —

"Harry, we haven't planted the garden yet."

"Vegetables. I want some excitement. Something new and different."

"Harry, you haven't been right since we lost the sheep."

"I saw twin fawns born this morning up on the summit in the madrones. They had legs the size of my little finger and they were slick as apple sap. I've been watchin' that big-bellied doe for a week, and by God, all of a sudden she squats, strains, and pops them out."

"You goin' to pop a hip joint back up in there one of these times and nobody will even know where to look."

Those were the best days. He went out at daybreak when dew dripped from the low grasses. He wanted to follow those fawns clear into next winter, sketch a few studies, and write a journal. He walked up the hogback to his fence, crossed through into the state park, then worked up eastward toward the sun's glow, climbing the ridges to the summit. It was a hard two miles. His breath whistled, he was sweating and his plastic hips ached, but he felt euphoric, young and light on his feet. He felt like laughing, like seeding the feminine fields, like roaring back down at the ocean curving into space.

He kept downwind of the patch of orange and green trees across the draw where the twin spotted fawns should be sequestered, and he moved very slowly, a long, careful approach. In time they might not be afraid of him, but now they were spooky and vulnerable. If he were greedy, or heavy-footed, he might destroy them.

He surveyed the madrone knoll for fifteen minutes and saw nothing. They must be sleeping. Fine with him. He had the whole mountain range and the broad tanker-dotted sea to look at while they napped.

But he smelled it. He guessed he sensed it even more than he smelled it. A taint. He waited an hour before admitting his dread that death was at work.

Pieces of the two ripped up and uneaten fawns were scattered through the lovely golden barked trees where the dogs flushed them out, caught them, and ripped them.

The doe had two defenses: to remain absolutely still or run crazier than anything else.

She was probably hanging around, down in the gulch circling, hoping the fawns had lain still since she tried to decoy the pack away, her bag would be stretched full of milk, her eyes wary, head up, hooves touching silently.

She would not recognize the shreds of her young.

This death was unspeakably hideous.

They were not coyote tracks, and they weren't cat tracks, they were tracks of a motley dog pack.

He'd had enough. They'd pushed and crowded and chased him clear to this summit in the only wilderness left to the virile independent master of a mountain.

Dusty rifles, cradled on a walnut rack: the ought-six for long, hard shooting, the .44 magnum carbine for brush hunting, the surplus M-1 carbine for quickness, the old 30-30 saddle gun for reliable all around shooting, then the 22s for bluejays and gophers.

Planning the campaign, he asked himself if the dogs would attack. The answer was no, they wouldn't. If he yelled, they'd turn and run, otherwise they'd tear him to pieces and there was no otherwise in him.

Therefore, he shouldn't need the short automatic rifles. He needed the soft-triggered long barrel. The maple-stocked ought-six had an eight power scope, and with a little practice he could hit a rat at three hundred yards, a long way in that country. The ammunition was old, but still bright brass in cardboard boxes. He settled on 180 grain softpoint slugs.

In his mind's eye, he could picture the hunt. He decided right then that he must take them all.

He didn't want to just scare them. He wanted to exterminate them so that he wouldn't be dumping sheep or seeing fawns torn up next year.

In the morning he hiked down to a small bench near his fenceline, just above Darvey's place. Darvey wasn't up yet, and Tony, his poodle, didn't bark. He didn't bark because he was gone. Harry scouted the area and found the ground where the dogs met, just a little meadow, fine for a frolic. Then talley-ho, off they go! Plenty of tracks and signs.

They'd take a natural course, and follow his road a ways. He tracked them on up to where they cut left at the next switchback, and that got them away from his house. He saw the old deer-run they followed and kept on their trail. His scent wouldn't bother them much when they came looping across next day. Now on a bare ridge in the open country, they were free of man. They used that bare ridge to go into the higher hills.

The trail became indistinct, because from here on there were rabbits, coons, foxes, deer, bobcats. The dogs changed their way of going according to the animal they flushed out and ran. Sooner or later they'd reach the summit though, and he had to plot them between this bare hogback and the top ridge to set his ambush.

He knew different areas where, if he could catch them right, he'd have them concentrated long enough.

No hurry. Half of it was the plan and stalk. He went on home and set up a bottle at two hundred yards to blow it away with the silky Remington trigger.

In the afternoon he was high up enough to where he could see that bare ridge down below, and noticed a sort of cul-de-sac burned over area across a gulch from him. A hundred yards. Once in that open spot they couldn't go any higher because of a cliff and a rockslide. It was a great place for them to chase game into. But best for him, there was no brush or forest cover to hide them. Say about three hundred yards of total exposure. That made his arc from a hundred to two hundred fifty yards. An Afghan could run an eight second hundred easy. He had about twenty seconds at most to shoot six to ten dogs.

The Remington was bolt action, accurate but slow. Best if he could move his position closer down to pen them in, make them come at him to escape.

He climbed on over, making sure there would be cover all the way, and found the right spot. Once there, he had them in the bag and they'd have to make a run at him to get out, but they wouldn't, they'd panic and either jump off the cliff or circle crazy until they were all down.

Just in case, he'd bring the .44 hog gun loaded and ready, too. The Remington only held six cartridges.

He built a rifle rest of an old log which looked natural enough, and he checked the fire lane, making sure he could cover all of it. They'd roar by with mad eyes and crying throats, hot for the kill.

Now he had to wait long days and nights while they hunted.

He listened as they circled one way or another, coming up the hill, and beyond. He carried the two rifles fully loaded and his binoculars, nothing else.

He became an expert on wild dogs, but their patterns were so accidental he had to trust chance. They didn't leave for the hills at any particular time, and sometimes they'd stay out two or three days, living off their kills.

In the next week he had long looks at them and maybe once or twice he could have killed one.

There were always at least six, sometimes nine. A pair of them, the Irish setters, he recognized as belonging to a retired movie star whose house was four miles down the coast.

They romped and played in the tall wild oats, happy clowns, beautiful, grand, powerful friends until they scared out some small creature that transformed them into yipping, snarling predators. There was nothing genteel, no hint of the dilettante, only pure, pure savagery.

Luck was with them and against him. They were not led into the old bare burn. Somehow the rabbit or bobcat they'd be chasing would turn away, seeming to know that to enter that path was to be trapped.

While he waited, he wondered if he should try for another flock of sheep. He wondered if he'd have to leave the coast when those dogs were dead and their owners came at him in concert. People had been run out of Big Sur for less. He wouldn't answer them. He'd say the wilderness was beautiful and cruel. He wondered about packs of men who set upon another man for a cause: abortion, free love, democracy, cockfighting, religion, atheism, bullfighting, human rights, taxes, money, sex.

The metaphor of the dog pack was too obvious, too sickening.

The awful question had to come: who was he to judge the killers? Had he not abandoned reason, too? Was he not just as dedicated in arranging this massacre as that pack of dogs was dedicated to killing? And yet came that final back-against-the-wall stubborn conviction when you said I don't know, I don't care, this is the line I have drawn and I will not back up. Maybe he was crazy as a bedbug, but he meant to kill that mess of dogs no matter what.

Lot of time to think, sitting there concealed on his promontory like God, waiting for the right accident to happen. And the country was so beautiful in its colors, the kindly breezes, the horny perfume of spring flowers and grasses, and the bright flows of finches and the ancient wind rovers, the redtail hawks, routinely culling the dumber rabbits.

Out at sea, beyond Point Sur, a pair of white fishing boats bobbed over the reefs, they too preying.

He was tired, vexed with nine days of patience. Why not fold up the tent and accept the condominium with all the grace a fifty-eight year-old mountain man retains?

On the tenth day, at dawn, again he took his stand. He felt pretty sure the dogs had gone home the day before. They'd be as rested as he was weary, but then again, it might just be his day for a change.

Fox sparrows and juncoes worked around in the brush, and the wonderful flush of golden rose filled the sky behind Mount Manuel.

He heard the little yip of greeting far down below. His ears tuned in like a radio telescope on an invisible planet. An answering little bark filtered out of the redwood canyon. They were making their meet.

He dared not pray to heaven to bring them to him now, but he had his binoculars trained on the first open spot on the lower trail. If they were coming, they'd pass there soon. They never made much noise down that far when they first started to prowl.

The rifles were both loaded. He was ready whenever they were. The burn area was empty. If they missed his ambush today, he'd have to start hunting them one at a time, even though he knew that wasn't a solution, only vengeance.

He saw them through the glasses, coming single file. Their leaders were Pattimar's golden Afghans. But they didn't look like choreographed leaves now, they came tall and alert, their muscles hot and the wild blood roaring. They were the way dogs ought to be and were before man made them his best friend and humbled slave.

Indeed, they were transformed into splendid animals of natural beauty and power. The setters had come along, too, ranging, heads low for scenting. Bright, copper red, they could be Sioux on the scout a hundred years ago, so real they were in their environment. Then came old Peacepipe drifting by like a proud hunter, amazing the new agility and fire in him. And there was true Tony striding along like a fancy French paladin, and spotted Roger went bouncing by. There was Tootie Wisenberg's police dog, and Phelp's Saluki coursing like an Arab sheik, and Beeman's collie, low to the ground. One more, a big, black dog, part Airedale, part Dane. Harry didn't know him. A newcomer. And there were no more. He was relieved. Old Rocky, Sam Hodman's dog wasn't in that gang of rangers. He had a few minutes to wonder if perhaps Rocky was close enough to the old pioneer people so he knew better. Rocky, like his lion-killed Lab Poky, knew his job was to defend the homestead, not to attack outside nature.

Eleven big dogs, hot to trot. Chances were three to one against their going into his trap, but he had the sense that they would go, the same sense you had when pitching horseshoes and as the shoe left your fingers, you knew it would be a ringer.

He dropped down behind his rock. The breeze came from the west, in his favor.

A yip, a bark, and another, and they were in full cry, on to something he couldn't see. They were nearly half a mile below in the redwoods, but it was something bigger than a rabbit.

He saw the big doe. Her ears were back and she jumped crazy on the snapping springs of her incredible legs, dodging from one side to another, trying to use the cover and simply beat her pursuers with her abandoned race, willing to break legs and neck in her mad flight, because it was all she had to save her life, but dear God, the Saluki was fast!

Nothing in that country could outrun the silky cousin of the Greyhound. The Saluki couldn't bring down the doe, because she was too light, her head and jaws too small. She was bred for running small desert animals and the doe was simply too big for her, but the bigger dogs, slower but stronger, would arrive.

Jesus, what a time they must have had with his sheep. It must have been over in seconds. The racing Saluki should be brought down first.

Straggling, baying, barking, the rest of the pack stayed closer together, not bothering to figure out or follow the zigs and zags, just hanging on to the course of the Saluki.

A concerted, fearful, frightening din of dogs, powerful natural forces on the run, hooked into their basic primordial flood, and they wanted hot smoking blood.

The doe tired. She could go another mile maybe, but she'd need luck to lose this mob. Even without the Saluki they could take her. Should he try to save the doe at the expense of the ambush? He decided she must live or die on her own, as if he were not there.

But he was coiled up into his own spring. He had the ought-six slung over his shoulder. He had the .44 in his left hand and he crouched, screened, studying the doe's moves. Would she go into the bare burn?

They were only three hundred yards below him and cutting across to the next knoll. She was avoiding his spot, but suddenly the Saluki nipped her hocks, and she swerved back, out of control, an insane deer leaping valiantly, crazily, veering off, coming up the cross ridge, up and onto the rocky ridge-back that could go nowhere except into the bare burn!

He started off, moving fast.

The doe and the Saluki were going up and in as he dropped down to cut them off, timing it to the second. He counted them as they raced by, tongues flapping, ears flattened, screaming in pursuit, their doggy eyes mad with heat and passion for blood. Two pretty Afghans going all out, the Dalmatian, two setters side by side, Laurie's police dog, the poodle, the collie, the black Dane-Airedale, and good old stoned Peacepipe dragging up the rear. He passed by so near, Harry could have tripped him from his hideout, but he was as intent on death as any of them, murder gripping every hot animal line and fiber of his body. Harry crossed over to the log, set the .44 aside, laid the loaded ought-six across the log, snapped off the safety, and crouched on one knee, sighting in . . . what should he sight in . . . where was the fast Saluki . . .? A pack of crazy dogs tearing a big doe to pieces, reds, whites, blacks, mottled splotches, tearing, and blood on their big fanged muzzles snarling at each other, the doe disappearing beneath their crushing slaughter.

He fired into the entire mess, high enough to hope to miss the deer, and time stood still for all of them with the stunning, echoing report. The blunt crush of that 180 grain bullet tearing through dogs, blowing the Dane-Airedale completely end over end out of the group, and spinning Roger, the Dalmatian, into a black and white blur. There were only fragments for eye recording, swirling around and round, confused, and Harry wasn't waiting to pick out the Saluki, he fired again at a tangle, and blew out the Saluki anyway, a golden floating of fine-boned screaming, O God, they screamed against death! The doe was up, hobbling, bleeding, then down again from a heavy weight of weariness and weakness. The dogs were aware of terror slamming in from somewhere. He levered in another big cartridge and laid his crosshairs on a running setter, put it right on his silky red head and blew it off with the feathersoft trigger, and now they were going round and round in a mad carousel of color, all howling in pain and panic, and he took out the other three-legged Irish Setter, the bullet so heavy it lifted him and threw him. Now Peacepipe, a lean, gray grizzly force, raced toward the cliff, and Harry followed with the scope, carefully moving the crosshairs across his body to the shoulder. He dodged over a rock and Harry followed again, taking too long maybe, but he could do nothing less, and had him again, moved the sight over to the gray muscled shoulder and gently squeezed the trigger. Harry didn't watch him go, but levered in another shell. There went the police dog, very quick and nimble, looking for cover, ready to leap into the canyon, and Harry helped him over with the soft-nosed bullet, smashing him out into space howling and convulsive and a hole the size of a coffee cup blown out the ribs. Harry tried next to catch the collie, but she was quick, too, and she dodged and his magazine was empty. He brought out a handful of shells and as he watched the Afghans, the collie and Tony, the bloody-faced poodle came together in their crazy gyrations, desperate for escape.

Somehow they flashed to each other that there was no way to go except out, and maybe the Afghan bitch gave the command. She was smart as anything, and still strong. In the silence of the empty rifle, they converged, they blended again, and turned, somehow making and absorbing a signal, a declaration: charge.

His big rifle was still unloaded. He saw the Afghans tense, shift, and spin, and in mighty side by side leaps they led the other two directly at him. Harry grabbed up the .44. They came fast as wind, a flowing force quicker than quail or pheasant. Incredibly swift in their fear.

He had no time to yell. He rose to an easy stand. Now he wanted them to know the gray wolf on the mountain. He gave them nothing else. Carbine to his shoulder, quick sighted on the rising, catapulting pair, he smacked each Afghan backward with big, blunt bullets. They died silently, instantly. The white pompom poodle had no choice but to keep coming on his flank. Harry quick hit him in the belly, good enough to hold him for awhile and the collie, trying to dodge around, almost made it, but today Harry was letting nothing by, and he blew her front leg off. He reloaded and then he blew her heart out. He turned back to Tony and shot him through the head, quick-stopping his scream.

There was still shrieking over in the tangle. He checked each bloody body until he found the police dog gutshot, crawling slowly, yellow eyes staring at him, a moan from her frothing jaws, and he punched her between the eyes. Thump. Gone. Rot.

The doe tried to scramble away. Too much blood to tell how badly she was hurt. She might be hamstrung, she might be belly ripped, or she might bleed to death from the gashes in her throat. Her life was her own.

They were all as dead as his sheep, dead as the fawns, dead as Oswald and Jack.

Very weil. He would not leave Apple Pie Ridge. He knew where he stood.

Slinging the empty ought-six on his shoulder, he unloaded the .44 and he followed the trail that would take him home.

6.

Fire

HEAT WAVES HAZED off the fisted hills knuckling down from the ridge to the western sea, and the sun lowering into that red chopped ocean seemed suspended just over Point Sur Rock like a great fireball, cooking the coast through every degree of its massive arc.

His instinctual fear of fire exacerbated by that searing sun, Harry came into the rocky barnyard, his shirt wet and unbuttoned, the mottled hair on his chest marked with rivulets of sweat, his weather-burned face brown as hot sandstone. Leaving his brushhook in the barn, he walked to the house thinking of cold beer, an easy chair on the shady side of the porch, and his boots off.

Greta waited for him by the door. She wore a fresh, cool cotton dress.

"Something wrong?" he asked. "Smell smoke?"

"No," she smiled girlishly, an unusual expression for a middle-aged ranchwoman. "I thought we might walk out to Big Oak Point and watch the sun set."

"Oh, hell," his big shoulders slumped, "why didn't you give me a hint this morning?"

"It's just another anniversary," she laughed at his downcast face.

Walking side by side down a lane of long, hot shadows, he tall and rangy, she short and slightly bowlegged, they resembled comic cowboy characters, except that each seemed to radiate a protectiveness over the other, the harmony and stewardship of enduring marriage.

"How many this time?" he asked.

"This is the thirtieth."

"By God, I always swore I'd never stay married thirty years to the same woman."

"Ah, you," she smiled.

The great oak stood at the western edge of the ranch in a field of dry wild oats that stepped off into the valley a thousand feet below. Years ago, Harry had built a redwood bench under the serene sheltering tree where the outlook was more spectacular than any other on the ranch. He'd have built their house here if he'd been able to find water for it.

"Sun's as red as your hair," he said, slumping to the bench, his own brush of hair as white as the distant surf slanting against the shore.

The sun seemed to disappear like the popping of a tiny red bubble, one moment there was fire, the next moment orange flaked water and a crimson sky.

"Gosh, Harry," she stirred from her thoughts, "we used to make love here in the wild oats in the spring."

"I remember," he said somberly, and then smiled. "You were an animal."

"Ready?" she asked, rising.

"Ready for what?" he pretended panic.

"Silly," she grinned and took his hand. "Ready for your dinner? I baked a cake." As they walked back through the pink and purple crepuscular light she said, "They been a nice thirty, Harry."

"We got a ways to go yet, lady."

Next morning, the same sun burned like a red shouldered bull over Mount Manuel, and Harry spent the morning cleaning out the failing springs in the high canyon. The stream had never gone dry in all these years, but his sense of the country told him the drought would not break, and nature served her own extremes first, and the homesteader must do his best.

Usually Harry could kid the Forest Rangers along as they performed their make-work routines, but that afternoon when the beer-bellied supervisor in his green uniform, a .357 magnum hitched to his hip and a nameplate pinned to his pocket that read Rudolf T. Seward, started ragging him about the fire clearance around the various ranch buildings, he snarled back, "Look, Rudy, either they're cleared your goddamned silly thirty feet, or they're irrigated green, or they're in the canyon where nothing will burn anyway."

"I'm just telling you the rules." The paunchy ranger, his cheeks and nose disfigured by broken blood vessels, filled out the citation. "You've got ten days to do it."

"Buzz off, Rudy," Harry flared, "and if you come back, leave your popgun at home."

"It's your neck, old timer," the ranger shrugged, and climbed back into his new green truck. "I'm just doing my job."

"What is it, Harry?" Greta called from the garden, diverting him enough to let the ranger depart.

"That goddamned Rudy, calling me an old timer. Those punks think they know something when they put their goddamned slave's uniform on."

"Rudolph the red nosed ranger?" she smiled. "He's harmless."

"I guess I'm gettin' meaner'n a blind rattlesnake in a bagfull of bobcats," Harry said. "It's the heat and dryness."

"Sure, August is always crazy," Greta said.

"You know damned well all the buildings are cleared good, besides the firebreak I been cutting all summer across the hill. They don't give me any thanks for that."

"Once it rains, everything will be okey-dokey."

He suddenly realized she was deliberately soothing him down and he felt angry that his manhood should be wrapped up in cotton, as though he were a maniac that had to be confined in a padded cell.

"Bull," he growled.

The ring of the telephone cheated him of more temper. "It ain't right," he mumbled to himself as she answered the phone. "Nowadays a man can't have balls. Soon as he snorts, they geld him."

"Harry," she called sharply, "they're calling from Australia."

"Now what?" he grumbled, knowing his big sons wouldn't call all that way except to bring bad news. What a time! Kids working in construction down under when they could just as well be home working on the ranch. They weren't even kids anymore. Mike was twenty-six. Pretty little Julia, the youngest, married to an engineer in Saudi Arabia, was nineteen now.

"Hello." He spoke into the receiver.

"Hi Dad," Mike's voice had changed somehow, adapting to the Aussie pickle-nose speech. "Or I reckon I should say Grand-dad."

"What's that?" Harry's orneriness melted. "What's that you say, Mike?"

"Got a big fat boy, ten pounds, six ounces, named Harry Mike."

Tears welling from his eyes and joy in his throat, Harry couldn't speak.

"Gail's doing fair-dinkum, and the baby has red hair like Momma's."

Suddenly Harry knew that ten thousand miles away his son was crying, too. All of the men in the family stood reserved and strong until such a wonder released them.

"We want you and Momma to come over. We're thinking of buying a ranch on the coast."

"Gosh, Mike, I can't leave on account of the drought. Maybe Momma can come over though." Harry felt exhausted and wonderful.

"You want to talk to Sam?"

He spoke to his second son, and then was passed over to young Jerry who had been so close to being a juvenile delinquent, Harry had sent him over to his brothers for his own good. They were working hard, saving money, had found a beautiful piece of land much like Apple Pie Ridge where the weather was mild enough to grow avocadoes.

At last he handed the phone over to Greta and went out under the oak tree to pace in the shade, and think about the family. A grandson. Harry. Maybe he ought to feel like a tottery old grampa, but he didn't. He felt as strong as a bull.

"That call must have cost them a fortune," he said when Greta came out. "You going?"

"Me? To Australia?"

"Michael wants you."

"But who's to do the canning? And where's the money to come from?"

"I can scare up the money all right."

"No, no, you keep that money in the bank. You never know what's going to happen."

A lonely feeling clawed at Harry's chest that evening when the molten sun finally set and heat winds came gusting down off the mountains. He missed his strong boys. Even though they wrangled and sometimes even yelled at each other, there was a certainty that they were all of one rock. But now it seemed so hopeless. Now they weren't coming back.

A merciless morning sun seared the hills that had not cooled in the night. Tall woody mesquite and wild lilac, dry as desert bones, crackled on the slopes though there was no wind.

Nothing a man can do about seismic shocks, nor landslides either, once they get moving, Harry thought, but what about fire? The red nosed ranger enforcing thirty foot clearances knew nothing of fire in these sharp shinned hills. Thirty feet was flea scratch in a steep high brush fire.

The only protection a man could devise was a bare lane to set back-fires against, and he had already broken his back at clearing out a swath of thick brush below the ranch buildings. Best thing today would be to loaf around the swimming pool, keep cool, and rest easy.

"Harry," Greta called. "You want anything from town?

Penny's coming down with a friend."

"Ask her to bring Moe along, too."

Out in the corral he played with the colt awhile, just making him his horse, teaching him how to handle his feet, how to mind a rope, a swat on the haunch, a look at the back teeth. Billy was a pussy cat, Harry thought, spraying the botfly eggs on his hocks, he knows me inside out. Most horses would have spooked away from the hissing spray.

"You're a hell of a colt, Billy."

The sorrel sighed and rattled as Harry climbed over the plank fence and hosed fresh water into his trough.

How the hell does a botfly know enough to come all the way up on the ridge to find my colt? Harry wondered. Nature was always such a baffling mother.

He heard the Volkswagen a minute before Penny came driving around the corner.

Just opposite from her little sister Julia, sometimes Penny brought home a gaiety, most times she brought the ache of a runaway obsolete flower child and sometimes she just brought herself, tired, beaten and needing the touch of the ranch.

And maybe half the time, depending on her mood, she'd bring Moe, her black son, Harry's first grandchild, a boy that needed the ranch stability more than any other Harry knew.

Tall and saucy, with long hair as black as hard coal, Penny unfolded from the little car, kissed Harry and, squealing with a delight that seemed out of character, she introduced her friend. "Rachel, this is my pop, Harry McAlister."

"Pleased to meet you," Harry took the chubby blonde girl's hand and tried to see some depth in her eyes. Instead, he met a cement smile.

A lot shorter than Penny, her whole person seemed to be compressed. Short arms, pinched shoulders, stubby neck, big head and blond hair starting low on her forehead. Other than that, in a workshirt and a pair of shapeless twill pants he couldn't tell much.

Moe climbed out of the back seat and leaped into Harry's arms, giving him a hard hug, and Harry tousled his kinky afro and kissed the boy's cheek.

"We came down to cool off," Penny said. "Hotter'n a pistol in town."

Harry looked at her closely. She looked heathly. When she came home like a poisoned cat he hated it, but then, bless her, if she just came home for a quiet pleasant time, that's what the ranch was all about.

"Pool is just right," Harry said. "I figured to go there and pant in the shade like a hot lizard."

Rachel laughed. A pretty smile he thought, a false tooth but not afraid to show it. He noticed a scar that twisted the corner of her mouth down, and another on her nose.

But what was it in those clean blue eyes that reminded him of something, someone else, some other time? A remembrance or a challenge?

"Come on in," Greta greeted them. "You're just in time for lunch. And Moe, there's fresh grapejuice for you."

They nibbled at openfaced sandwiches outside by the pool and chattered routine gossip.

Rachel was going to college, studying urban planning and working part-time as a barmaid in a Fisherman's Wharf saloon.

"You ought to try something like that," he told Penny. "There's still the money left from your sister's college account."

"Better just donate little Julia's money to my dentist," Penny smiled. "I'm a little old for book learning."

"How old are you, Rachel?" He addressed her bluntly and his eyes held hers.

"Twenty-one."

He paused, ready to speak, but a flicker in those iron blue eyes touched him, baited him, delaying his reply. "You look some older," and stuttering then in confusion, "I don't mean you look older, or as old as Penny, only you look older than twenty-one."

"Ages are strange things anyway," Rachel replied, looking away. "They don't mean anything to me."

"Hell, Pops, I'm only twenty-four," Penny said, her face brittle.

"Yes, it's the times are getting away from me," he said,

puzzled at his confusion. Better he just shut up.

What was the mystery, what was the tragedy, coded and beckoning, behind those blue eyes? Why did he even think of it? He'd seen dozens of young people with those same window glass eyes and never bothered before.

Greta seeemed to be talking a lot, filling in the long gaps of silence. " . . . and the nasturtiums are suffering because they're not really up to any kind of heat the way it's been lately . . ."

The great sunball blasted. The brushy hillsides crackled with heat.

"Let's go swimming," Moe begged.

It was the custom, established by the kids from the time they built the pool together, that they didn't bother with swimsuits. Greta never quite grew accustomed to it, and always wore something designed to hide her matronly curves.

Rachel revealed breasts more fat than firm, trunk thick and short, frizzy pubic hair covered a clenched fist and her broad butt continued solidly down to her knees. She was a dumpling, built like a large dwarf. Some terrible genetic mismatch had produced the body, yet her long whiskey colored hair that started from a widow's peak fell to her waist in a beautiful cascade, her smile stayed steady but her eyes contained a tunnel of sorrow he couldn't fathom. Somewhere behind that low forehead was a child's loving mind and a sensitivity that needed to be appreciated, revealed, and reborn.

He felt a sense of protection for the dumpling and then he felt an unaccustomed stirring in his loins that embarrassed him. He blushed and made a flat dive into the pool to shock his body into some sense.

Good Lord, Rachel was younger than his daughter!

And he was old as the hills!

Still, what was this strange connection that shook his emotions, that called up a reaching empathy, that joined their eyes in an understanding he didn't understand.

Calm, uncaring, she lay on her stomach, sunning her frogskin textured backsides. When she walked, she must chafe her legs all the way down to her knees, he thought.

Why should he be thinking about the inside of her thighs? Harry, for Christ's sake, get off it! he commanded. But in another minute his gaze had drifted off to the young woman with the long golden hair.

He noticed that she didn't smoke, but covertly chewed her fingernails down to the raw.

She seldom spoke. He wondered if there was any thought inside that symmetrical face. She was really too young to know anything yet, he decided. Her taciturn manner showed a rare sense of modesty, her small replies to his general questions, he considered a courtesy.

She rolled over and spread her legs to let the sun in.

He decided he should be helping Greta pick tomatoes. Some strange spongy thing was growing inside his chest, up into his throat, a choking swelling thing he didn't understand, and not understanding, he was unable to hold it back.

Maybe, he thought for an instant, maybe I'd like it. I'm man enough.

Slipping his long tightly muscled legs into blue jeans and leaving his shirt behind, he went barefoot to the garden.

"You know anything about that girl?" he asked Greta.

"One of Penny's friends is all I know. Why?"

Harry stopped to pick a ripe tomato. "She just seems familiar, like I knew her from somewhere."

They ate dinner on the cool side of the deck.

"It's the driest spell we've ever had," Greta said.

"And maybe the hottest," Harry added.

"Plenty of water in the stream?" Rachel asked, looking straight into him again with those unreadable challenging eyes.

"Enough, if we use it right."

The night didn't cool, and the moon rose big and orange over Mount Manuel. They sat in silence, listening to night sounds, feeling cooler as heat gusts came down off the slopes, and the moon, like a magic orb, beckoned all the lovers of summer to rise and sing.

"Ready for bed, Moe?" Greta asked.

"Ready," the boy said. "Good night Grampa."

"Night, son," Harry said from a moonlit dream.

No one else spoke. Greta and the boy were gone. The cicadas sang, the crickets shrilled, a pair of owls worked the dry hillside, a Poorwill cried, the grand moon flooded its light over the ridge.

"I think I'll hit the sack," Penny said. "You know where your room is?"

"Sure," Rachel said, "I'll cut out pretty quick."

"Me, too," Harry said, knowing he lied.

When they were alone, the silence stretched a million miles into another time and space. "You're so young to know so much," he said to the moon.

"I don't know anything."

"Somehow I see so much depth, so much dimension deep inside you. Like if you set your mind to it, you could move the whole country, the whole continent."

"Really?"

"It's a strange feeling. I don't often pay much attention to Penny's friends. They're usually too dumb."

"Thanks." Her low voice held a throb in its measure he hadn't noticed before.

He cast about in his mind what it was he wanted.

Yes, surely yes, it was required he should love this neglected girl. No one else would. She needed a well rounded and mature man, otherwise she'd never be fulfilled. What harm? Help her along, bolster her confidence. She couldn't help it if her body was out of scale.

"I'm entire," he said after awhile into the moony night, "and Greta and I are more like old pals now."

"Yes," she said in her low voice.

"I mean, I'm not a philanderer or anything, but I'm thinking about you."

"Go ahead," she chuckled, "think all you want."

"I mean, I've got some years on me. Maybe you'd be offended." Christ, he didn't want to talk that way but that's the way it came out.

"I'm not offended."

After awhile he couldn't help himself. "Let's go to your room."

"OK," she said. "Why not?"

He marveled that she could succumb so quickly and easily. The lump in his throat had almost choked him into silence, and as he followed her dumpy walk down the deck to her bedroom, he felt like a demon floating on a ribbon of fire.

She must be starved for love, he thought. With that misshapen body, no doubt the young bucks passed her by. They wouldn't ever see the unique quality that shone deep inside her slate blue eyes.

She lay on the bed and kicked off her twill trousers and the transparent brief that sketched her crotch. He unbuttoned the man's shirt she wore and she slipped out of the sleeves to lie like a bowl of cream before him. She tasted like salt and sleet and candlelight. Quiet as an apple tree in autumn she patiently waited and waited.

With a groan, he realized that she hadn't moved, hadn't responded, hadn't felt his passion.

"I'm sorry, Rachel," his voice came out thick and confused. "I couldn't help myself."

"It's OK," she slipped out from beneath him. "I don't get off anyway."

"Never?"

"Nope. It's OK."

"Look, Rachel," he said, "I'm not a man that messes around much but you're special to me. I'll do better."

"OK," she said. "Just don't make no big deal."

In the morning, Greta seemed quiet, but then there wasn't much to talk about except the unrelenting heatwave.

Rachel went along with him to feed the colt. He noticed she was quick with her hands, her stubby arms muscular, her stooped shoulders powerful.

In the hay mow he embraced her in a wave of passion and

her methodical tongue drove him crazy.

He tried to go even slower this time, touching and stroking her body, holding himself back, until as he controlled the pace of his body consciously, overcontrolling, hoping to bring her to a climax, he felt his own sex fail, and the more he tried to bring himself up, the more miserable his embarassment.

"I'm sorry," he groaned.

"Nothing to it," she smiled, "I can get you off." And quickly working on him with her mouth she brought him to his own crazy release.

He looked down at her steady face, only a trace of wetness in the corners of her mouth.

She smiled, "Bodies are just bodies."

"Don't you feel anything for me?"

"Don't get too heavy, Harry," she said, slipping on her pants and buttoning her shirt.

"Harry!" Greta called from the yard. "Telephone."

Later in the day, when they were all in the pool, he felt Rachel's soft body brush his own and he wanted her again, but Penny and Moe were splashing about on innertubes and Greta sat on the side, her blue veined legs dangling in the pool, and in anguish he swam underwater away from them all.

He thought Penny was looking at him oddly, and teasing him more than usual, and he tried to play with Moe to burn up the time to darkness.

To give the boy confidence, Harry tossed coins into the shallow water and encouraged him to dive and find them with his eyes open.

"Maybe tomorrow, I'll teach you a simple side stroke, Moe," Harry said.

"I can swim already, Grampa," Moe said.

"Even an old dog can learn new tricks," Penny said, an odd half smile on her dark features.

He blushed, his whole body flooded red, and he sank underwater where they couldn't see.

He hadn't ever thought about the making of dinner, Greta just always did it, but for the first time in thirty years, there was nothing cooking in the kitchen and nothing on the table.

"No dinner?" Harry asked, worried.

"Too hot," Greta said. "There's coldcuts and cheese in the fridge, and bread and crackers in the pantry."

He thought she was making some good guesses and wrongfully trying to punish him without any evidence.

He had another chance with Rachel that night, but he couldn't excite the golden tomboy into anything more than a casual movement.

"Nothing?" he begged.

"Don't worry about it." She cocked her head and made a pretty smile.

He ran his big old hand through the length of her soft hair and said, "We've got to take a trip or something."

"Whatever," she said.

Next morning, Penny was on the phone and Rachel was off by herself. Greta fixed the simplest of breakfasts.

"Another scorcher," Harry said.

"Makes the corn grow," Greta replied, studying her coffee.

"You going to visit the boys?" he asked.

"You want me off the ranch, I'll go."

"I just want you to do what you feel like doing," he said humbly.

"Okey dokey." She made a smile.

About noon, Penny came out to the barn. "There's a couple friends coming up if it's OK."

"Sure, the more the merrier," Harry lied.

"They're college guys," Penny added, sinking Harry's proud flagship and making his stomach grind in pain.

Still, in that awful heat on the crackling hills, a man couldn't go out and dig a posthole, or chop brush, without inviting a heatstroke. And if a man builds a swimming pool, why shouldn't he use it?

The girls lay naked on their towels, and Moe threw sticks in the pool for the young Lab who liked to swim.

Hearing the car coming up the road, Harry felt an awful dread of seeing Rachel with any man of her style and vigor and age. Damn, damn, damn, he accused himself, if I'd just worked a little harder, done better, had more time . . . .

Slipping on a short robe, Penny went to the driveway. Greta dangled her feet in the pool and, wearing dark glasses, read a book.

He couldn't comprehend it at first. His mind reeled as the tall one and the short one shook his hand, greeted everyone and took the clothes off their black bodies. Somehow, in spite of his tan, Harry felt very white.

The young men were fit and slim, their movements seemed to pace a syncopated music built into loose joints and young muscles. Harry felt his knees crack, and his shoulders creak when he dived from the log above the pool.

And Moe quickly adapted to their looseness, the dance in his own blood sensing the racial rhythms of Africa.

The boys complimented Harry on the organic self sufficiency of the ranch and its beautiful position, its vista, and lookouts.

Rachel called the shorter one Tommy right away, and spoke of past events Harry couldn't interpret. The tall one played it light and easy with Penny.

All his life, Harry had felt black men were underdogs, and he had believed he would back any underdog immediately. So he loved and elevated his grandson, Moe. Moe was born an underdog, his unknown father was born an underdog. Now the black man, the underdog, was taking his girl. Harry's spirit writhed, impaled on his manhood, impaled on his conscience, impaled on his own good sense.

He couldn't hate the black men. He just loved Rachel to the point of an agony breaking his chest, hoping against hope she would ignore the short one, love the old guy, the only man around who understood her deepest problems and would give his entire life and energy to fixing them.

Greta hardly tried cooking dinner. "It's just too hot in the kitchen," she said, but Harry could remember other heatwaves when she spent all day and half the night over a steaming canner.

At welcome nightfall, they sat out on the deck and Harry hoped the young men would soon go back to town, but they were in no hurry, their joints loose, their easy muscles hardly moving, their soft talk flowing along like a slow stream, their manhood moved by the common moon.

When it was obvious he was the extra one in the crowd, he rose and said goodnight as best he could, weeping in his heart that Rachel would be in black Tommy's arms in the moonlight. He was shaking when he crept into bed alongside Greta. Her long red hair lay loose and scattered on the pillow.

She wasn't asleep. He couldn't tell what she was thinking. At least, he justified himself, he had come to bed early.

"Harry," she said into the darkness, "I'm thinking of going to the beauty parlor."

"Whatever for?" he muttered.

"Get my hair cut and curled."

"Don't be silly. Your hair's the best there is."

"I'm thinking," she said.

Jesus, he thought, she can't compete anymore than I can.

At dawn he heard the black men's car start up and go down the hill.

He was used to Moe. He was used to Penny and her screwed up ways, but somehow he couldn't believe Rachel would make love to the black man the same way she did with him. His mind would not jump that hurdle, balked, and threw itself back in a destructive frenzy.

Later in the morning, silent, circles under his eyes, his smile gone, Greta looked at him for a long moment and said, "Harry, you're in over your head. What is it you want?"

"I don't know. I just don't know," Harry mumbled and, unable to face her anymore than that, turned away and went up in the redwood canyon to look at the dying ferns where there should have been a stream.

How could he mistreat Greta? She was his teammate, his help-meet, his other half.

How could he let that poor misshapen girl be lost to the blacks? They would put her on the street once they'd used her and doped her.

And what about Penny? Worse, what about little Moe? How could he ever function in this system?

"You like that guy?" he asked that night.

"Tommy? Sure, he's easy."

"Sleep with him?"

"Now, Harry," she giggled, "it's all right."

"What do you mean, all right?"

"I mean, it's just a casual relationship."

"Not to me," he said gloomily. "I can't compete against that kind of person."

"Harry," he heard Greta's voice from the darkness. "I think I'll go to bed."

His heart sank, a brassy taste filled his mouth. How had she sneaked up? How much had she heard?

The following overheated sunburnt morning, Greta said, "I'm going to visit the boys. You can get along okey dokey without me."

"Wait a second," he said, wanting her to leave, but wanting to feeling guiltless, too. "You don't have to go anywhere."

"You need some time to find out what you want."

"How long you going for?"

"I just may not come back, Harry," she said, trying to look him in the eyes and failing.

He felt weary. He felt wrinkled and withered and white haired and trembly.

She called the travel agent. A one-way ticket to Australia. No more, no less, even when the agent told her that if she didn't buy a return ticket, she'd have all kinds of problems with Australian authorities.

"Problems, problems, get me a one-way ticket," she said and hung up.

There was no joy on her face, only a single-minded stubbornness.

That night, when he managed to slip away, Rachel seemed evasive, resisting. "It's real tough, Rachel," he said. "I'm fighting ghosts, I'm carrying the world on my back."

"Don't bother."

She meant she didn't want to talk; she wanted to be loved but still she didn't respond. She took his passion and returned nothing except more anxiety, making him feel more and more a failure.

"Damn it, Rachel, I want to bring you off."

"Don't worry about it," she kissed his breast and sucked his nipple.

"We can start all over," he said. "I want to make you into a whole woman."

"Look, some people are better at some things than others are."

"You mean he's a better man than me?"

"Not exactly." She backed off.

The heat never stopped. Greta's tomatoes and corn burgeoned, but Greta wasn't picking anything, wasn't canning anything, she was packing her suitcases, selecting what she would take and what she would leave, her face determined, bleak, and critical.

"When are you coming back?" he asked humbly.

"When you decide what you want, I'll think about it."

"Greta," he said.

She packed a turquoise necklace he had given her years before.

Harry was a crushed man wandering in a storm of emotion he couldn't understand. He had lost Greta and the hope for a life with Rachel was dimmed by her opaque mentality, her steadfast affection for Tommy, the black youth.

"Rachel, I'm willing to give you everything I've got and help you make a success, but I want you for myself...."

"No way, Harry. I mean, Tommy's neat, too, and I don't want to hurt him."

"You mean a good old man is equated with a black kid?" he demanded.

"Harry, please, I can't handle it anymore," she wept.

"You bitch!" he growled.

"I'm free, too, Harry. I've got a life of my own."

He couldn't debate it.

At noon there was no lunch. Greta selected, piece by piece, what she would take and what she would leave.

A man in trouble ought to go up the canyon and chew on roots and rocks.

At ten minutes of noon on August eighth, he went down the deck to Penny's room to ask advice. She knew the problem. God knows, she knew everything there was to know about all kinds of men and their problems.

He should have knocked, but the door was ajar.

Tall Penny lay sprawled on the bed, staring at the ceiling with a fixed agonized expression, while Rachel equally nude, had assumed the position of lover, her knees between Penny's long legs, her face down, her hands kneading Penny's breasts.

He looked unseeing at the fat frogskin butt, the hands without nails working, the long whiskey-colored hair everywhere, foreshortened spine curved, sounds of sucking.

Enough. Oh, enough! he thought crazily, watching his daughter's hips rise against the face of his beloved, and fall, and rise trembling again.

He closed the door and sank in a vertigo of prolapsed pain. "I can't do it," he whispered.

The unspeakable vision burned like acid and fire into his brain. And the sorrow! The pain and grief inflaming his deserted being, spirit, soul, was too much, and he knelt by the door and spit dribbled out of his mouth, and his eyes burned.

He found himself rubbing the colt down, not yet wondering how he'd managed to go from the porch to the corral, talking to the animal, talking to himself. " . . . look here, Billy boy, you got to get yourself together. It's like the fairy tale and the witch puts a spell on. The whole damned ranch is under a bad spell . . . . I dunno, maybe it's the heat, maybe it's astrology, but for damned sure it's bad, and we got to shake it off some-how . . . . Got to get clean. Clean the whole ranch. I sure dunno what it's going to take to do it, but it ain't been right ever since that girl came . . . ."

But the sickness in his chest, the leaden pressure squeezing up from his bowels into his heart, blocked his thinking. He could only bring to mind an aching need to change the girl, recreate her. He thought he could save her from stupidity, frigidity, promiscuity, miscegenation, lesbianism, and he believed her soul was too precious to be abandoned because he was the only one who could see it and bring it to fruition. Nothing else mattered.

". . . Can't hardly compete against my own daughter. Can't compete against the black studs. But ain't none of them seen that fine light deep down inside her, they don't give a damn, they just want the ride . . . and she don't even know it herself, don't know she's got the light, a real greatness of spirit deep inside . . . if she could just bring it out she'd make the finest woman on this earth . . . ."

The colt nuzzled Harry's shoulder.

God, he felt old. What sorcery had she laid on him? His hands trembled, his shoulders pinched down. Why couldn't he see the sun blazing like a flare, why couldn't he smell the west wind that any other time would have sent a shiver of fear through him?

And what about Greta? When she left, he'd have the time to open the girl up and make her well, but it wasn't fair. Greta was a fine woman who deserved better treatment. Thirty years she'd been by his side, working her tail off for the family, and now would he run her off for the sake of a neurotic slut?

Questions! Questions! No hope of an answer.

By one o'clock the breeze from the west had picked up into a gusting wind that still could not relieve the midday heat.

He found Greta standing in the bedroom between two large suitcases. The expression on her face, quiet, dignified, thoughtful, solemn, belied the sorrow of their loss.

"I'm ready, Harry," she said.

"Can't you help me? Be patient awhile?"

"You got yourself into something outside of me, Harry. Do what you think is best."

"I don't want to lose you," he said.

"It's done," she said. "Done. And it's been grand, too."

"Greta," he said humbly, "don't be hard headed. I always figured you'd be around to bury me."

"Time to go, Harry. Like you always said, 'Time and tide tarry for no man.'"

"You want to say goodbye to Penny and Moe?"

"Not if I can help it."

He picked up the suitcases, a feeling of relief crashing like a cross-current against the rip tide of loss.

She stopped to look around, the big old house they'd built so long ago, the barn, Harry's workshop, the corral, the green pasture, the chicken house, greenhouse, sheepshed, all the trees and gardens, all the work they had concentrated on this ridge in the thirty years they'd been partners.

She opened the truck door, took a deep breath, and froze.

"Can you smell anything?" she asked quietly.

He sniffed the gusting wind. Suddenly his whole person reversed stance and rhythm. He breathed again the scent on that unholy wind, and his eyes widened with a rush of adrenalin. "Smoke," he said. "Jesus, it's to the west. Jesus H. Christ!"

"Maybe we better take a look, Harry." She hurried through the gate and across the pasture to the edge of the ridge where you could see all the way to the ocean.

"Smoke at the river mouth," Harry said.

A slight haze rose from a clump of alders close to the distant sea. "They'll hold it over there."

"The wind, Harry," she cautioned.

"It's gotta jump the river and the highway. I don't see how they can lose it."

"You're trusting the Forest Service?"

Still he didn't move, he wanted to read the signals that were hitting him, the smoke, the siren on the highway, the gusting wind picking up harder now, the dryness, the heat, the wind again.

She went to the truck and carried her suitcases back inside, and a moment later she brought Penny and Rachel and Moe out into the pasture.

More sirens keened on the wind, and they could see tiny

sparkling red lights flashing on the ribbon of blacktop far below.

"How far away is it, Grampa?" Moe stood close to Harry.

"From here to that smudge, I'd guess seven miles."

"That's a long ways," Penny smiled.

Rachel had nothing to say.

"My firebreak runs clear across the hill," he said. "I'll torch it off on the windward side if that fire jumps the highway."

"Water?" Greta murmured.

"We got enough water if the plastic pipe doesn't melt or the tank burn," Harry said, "and we've always got the swimming pool."

"Will they send us any help?" Rachel asked.

There was no answer.

They stood on the edge of the ridge and watched as the smudge expanded and more flashing lighted trucks came rumbling up the highway with their sirens and bullhorns blowing, turning into Molera Park and rolling off across the flatland toward the rivermouth.

"I'm going to fill the bathtubs," Greta walked back to the house.

"She's always worrying," Harry tried to joke.

"Will it get here, will it burn us up?" Moe clutched at Harry's hand.

"Not a chance. Look at all those fire trucks," Harry reassured the little boy.

The wind beat against them, rising in velocity, backing them into the lee of the sheepshed.

"Momma's not going?" Penny asked.

"Not while there's a fire out there," Harry said, seeing that image of the morning.

A twin engine plane came from the south and slowly circled the fire.

"Borate bomber," Harry said. "They're not taking any chances. These hills haven't burned in sixty years and the dead brush has piled up like stacks of kindling."

"Is it OK, Grampa?" Moe asked again in a small voice.

"Sure, boy, they can lay down a stream of fire retardant any time they want to."

Two planes now slowly circled the billowing smudge that lengthened flatly to the east.

All his dark thoughts disappeared when a fountain of flame broke out from the smudge.

"Goddamnit."

More than a few sparks, an inferno of burning debris showered from the smoke.

"Dad," Penny said, "we'll just be in the way."

"You want to go, better go now."

Rachel nodded, slack-jaw, shark mouth, stubby shoulders, her eyes fascinated by the building fire.

"I don't want to leave," Moe said.

One of the bombers made a slow dive, pulling out at the point of fire, releasing a rain of red dyed retardant.

"It's jumped the river," Harry said. "The sonsabitches."

The second bomber dived and dropped its retardant and flew away, leaving the sky vacant except for white and brown smoke aimed like a snake at their ridge.

"The wind has us nailed dead center," Harry said, "if it jumps the highway, we're going to eat it. You folks watch the main house, I'll be working on the rest of the buildings."

"We should clear out," Rachel said.

"Go ahead," Harry retorted.

Smoke obscured the whole valley. Somewhere under it men were being mustered to cut firebreaks, to run hoses from truck pumpers, to carry cans of water where the hoses wouldn't go. If only they would hold it at the highway, and failing that, send a couple fire trucks up here with strong young men.

Light white ash trickled out of the sky as Harry hurried to fill every water container he could find. The plastic pipe running down the canyon to the holding tank was too vulnerable. If it melted, there would be no water.

He drove his truck and Penny's car out into the green pasture in front of the house and he started hosing down the barn walls and roof, but already, because Greta was doing the same to the house, the water pressure was low and the spray he directed against the redwood walls seemed to dry off as fast as he could lay it on.

Flame and ash erupted from the timber along the highway and for a second he saw lines of stopped cars.

He ran to the house. Rachel and Penny were packing their little suitcases. Greta moved along the deck, wetting walls and roof with a hose.

"Gret," he yelled, "they've lost it. Get on the phone and yell for help. We need trucks, planes, helicopters, men, anything, and right now!"

He ran to the barn and found the colt nervously sniffing the wind. Harry was damned if he'd leave the colt confined in a death trap.

The ash that fell was darker, fresher, heavier, and hot. A holocaust would be roaring up the ridge on the beating wind.

Harry opened the gate and chased the colt down the back-road into the canyon where the deep redwoods were cool and there was still a dampness in the stream bed. After that, he decided, the horse had to take care of himself.

Thanking heaven that he'd not only had the hip operation, but had the time to rebuild the ruined muscles, he positioned buckets of water by each building.

Choking smoke at ground level now, and despite the ache in his side, he ran from place to place, throwing out trash, moving woodpiles, praying for the wind to change.

He thought he ought to light his backfire, but there was always a chance the main fire would be contained, the wind drop, some miracle, and he didn't want to jeopardize his neighbors, nor the forest and all the life it contained.

He delayed lighting the fire along the western firebreak.

He ran back to the house. Through sheets of gray blowing smoke he could see the lazy bombers circling overhead, looking for a target, waiting for orders from the fireboss, and Harry knew right then that they were lost.

He knew Rudy was incompetent and unreasonable, a bragging drunken bum who became fireboss by being noisy and lasting longer than anyone else.

He could picture Rudy right now, overwhelmed by firefighters wanting commands, needing decisions. And he knew that man had already crumbled. There would be no orders given in the next hour, the bombers would circle, the helicopters loaf around, the firetrucks pull back and wait, and nothing would be done to save poor beautiful Apple Pie Ridge or the wilderness beyond.

Greta spoke urgently into the phone. "We need help right now, yes, right now! No, we are not evacuated, girl, we are all up here at Apple Pie Ranch and need help immediately, urgently, please!"

She looked at Harry's haggard face and shook her head. "Girl, please get ahold of the head man and send help. I have to hang up."

"They're all mixed up, Harry," Greta said. "They don't think anyone's here."

"They must figure to just let it burn to hell and gone then, the rotten sonsabitches!"

"Come on big fella," she grinned and spontaneously gave him a hug, "We'll just give it a punch in the nose."

"I'm out at the buildings. Soak the house, but if you think you're losing it, yell. The house comes first."

"All right, Harry," she said, and he watched her hustle out on the deck, her knotted and bowed legs doing their best, and, grabbing a ladder, she crawled up on the roof while he ran to the outbuildings.

Fine cinders burned his lungs as he breathed deeper and harder, running from place to place, swatting at flying sparks with a wet sack, stamping them out when they hit the dry grass, but when he looked over his shoulder at the far ridge to the east, he saw the awful eating ulcer of a wind-carried fire burning on the side of that distant back ridge, and he knew they were surrounded by fire, the water line would burn, and it was just the beginning.

Nothing left to do except light the backfire. Running hard, he reached the clear break between the oncoming fire and the ranch buildings. He struck a match in a rat's nest on the windward side that flamed like hot dry tinder. With his shovel he carried embers on down the break, intentionally setting a wall of fire he hoped would creep against the wind to meet the rising, engulfing wave of burning brush and trees, a mammoth flame a hundred feet high fanned and whipped by the gusting wind, building of itself more wind, more heat, more intensity, more rolling flame.

He kept his backfire to the upwind side of the firebreak, but the wind was too strong. His backfire wouldn't move.

Knocking down sparks, he saw a great tongue of flame reach uphill, outflanking his firebreak, licking at the chicken house, and before he could run up the slope to release the flock, the chicken house was an inferno, incinerating the flock, scattering more fire, taking the old sheepshed with it, adding more fire, the heat so intense and the air so acrid and wasted, he fell to the ground, cussed, climbed to his feet again, and ran to save the barn.

A lifetime's heirlooms were stored in that barn. The black suit that he was married in was packed away in there somewhere, and the maple handled tools he had collected, and the copper moonshine still, and the boys' goods all stored away. Even half a box of dynamite was stored in the coolest spot beside the acetylene and oxygen tanks, the propane tank outside, the woodshop, the freezers full, the old trout poles and fine reels, the letters from his father, everything of their lives was in that big old redwood building.

A wall of flame surged like a hellish surf and rolled over the top of the ridge, knocking him down into ash and dust, and his face was black, and the roof of the barn already patched with fire. He tried the hose, but there wasn't enough pressure, and he might have stopped to breathe and sob, but the propane tank blew its safety and a howling plume of burning gas spurted from the valve and he thought in terror, it's going to go, it's going to blow up like a goddamned bomb! And he ran towards the house in a terrible terror that the tank would explode before he could reach Greta and the house and make his fight once and for all.

The sun stood like a ruby, fuzzy and indistinct through the

billowing smoke. And he could hear the planes circling slowly overhead, the bombers that might have saved the barn with just one pass, the helicopters that could have landed men and taken out the women, they were circling, just circling, waiting for someone to tell them there was a homestead and a human family dying just below.

He found Greta on the ladder and heard the truck's gas tank explode in the middle of the pasture. Over the roar of the flaming wind, he yelled, "Where's Moe?"

"I put him in the pool," she yelled into his ear.

"You go," he yelled.

"No!"

In a mad burst of passion, he pulled her roughly to him until a sense of tenderness reached from his spirit and he pulled back, looked into her good eyes, and kissed her softly. "I do love you, Greta. Now damn it, go!"

"Okey dokey, Harry."

"Damn it!" he yelled in frustration and despair. "Damn it to hell!" He grabbed the hose and leaped up the ladder to the roof in a pure and savage rage. He would not yield another inch! He would rather goddamned die on that roof!

And while Greta carried buckets of water from the pool to splash against the walls, he stood on top spraying the little peehole of water, all that was left. The roof only needed a spark to set it off in one big bang of fire. The redwood shakes he had split thirty years before were smoking and he traveled over the roof stomping at it and spraying the precious water as the great surf of flame roared over the top once more with such a hot and intense shock he was knocked to his knees. He lay on his stomach until it passed over and, crazed, he stood facing the firey wind and yelled: "You sonofabitch, you will not have my house. I will not move!" And he sprayed and rubbed the smoldering shakes with his raw hands and tried to hold it all together, minute by minute, until, pray god, the holocaust would pass by, but again the wall, the wave of greasewood, red and yellow fire, bloomed over the brow of the hill, lifted on a mighty gust of blowing ash and sparks, and again he was smashed down on his belly, trying to find air for his lungs so that he could rise and fight again and, standing, he turned to the wind and yelled, *"I will stun you with thunder, by god. I will drown you in my stinking piss, you shall not have my house! By god, I will beat you like a yellow dog! I am too old to make mad and this is too good a house for you to burn!"* And he sprayed the smoking shakes, and rubbed off the embers with his bleeding hands, staying there, not knowing he was raving like Macbeth, not knowing what he yelled, not the poetry or the pain, fighting from his rage and refusal to yield his house to any fist of flame.

Knocked flat again, he rolled down the pitch of the roof, his clothes so hot they would torch on a spark, but at the gutter of the roof, he held on, and tried for more breath, lungs sucking in air that held little oxygen, no life. On his knees once more, he thought the main heat of the wind and fire had changed. Yet he could see another fantastic wall of fire coming on a diagonal up the hill. It would cover the pool where his family waited.

There was no more water in the hose, all the buckets empty.

He crawled down the ladder like a wounded scarecrow and ran without hearing the firestorm, nor seeing the blowing ash, the burning outbuildings, the destroyed cars in the blackened pasture.

At the edge of the pool, they watched him, trusting his judgement, his leadership. Moe, Penny, Rachel, Greta. They crouched in the water, their heads covered by wet towels and sleeping bags, but their eyes were trusting him, all except Rachel whose eyes rolled in terror, whose scarred mouth leaked a faint ashen foam from each side. For a moment he had a crazy vision that he saw semen oozing out of her mouth and nose and eyes, but it was Greta who spoke to him. "Come in, Harry," she said quietly. "We've done all there is."

Overhead the planes cruised their idle circles. "Surely," he said, "they'll help us."

"No, Harry," she said, "they won't. They will only help themselves, you know. Come on in, Harry."

He couldn't. He'd be immobilized and he would never be able to move again if he stopped, but the oblique wave, the towering screaming surf of flame came over the ridge, held off from house and pool only because they were set back from the steep side hill and were granted a few feet of space.

Harry slumped. Slowly sinking to his hands and knees, he saw the others in the pool, their eyes big, their mouths all open and sucking at the air for oxygen that was not there and he remembered how fires had killed their victims as simple as that. Take away the oxygen for a couple of minutes and you've got a bunch of stiffs floating around for the Forest Service boys to fish out the next day and nod and say, they should have done this, they should have done that. And he heard the planes lazily circling overhead and then he felt Greta pulling at him, dragging him into the pool with the rest of them, holding a wet soaking towel over his head and keeping his head above water while they all gaped like goldfish in a bowl of week-old water, gaping silently, he the only one who knew why they were sucking so hard at ashes in the air, knowing there was no life in it, and he said *O god, give us some air,* and he felt a black hood coming down but he yelled, "I will not!" And raised his head and grabbed Moe to his body and slammed an arm around Greta, and yelled again at the waves of fire rolling up the ridge, "No!"

And then he slumped against Greta until sometime later, not long, she splashed warm poolwater in his face and said, "There's things to do."

The noise had dropped, the storming firewaves gone. He filled a bucket and followed Greta.

Hardly looking, he doused the water on a burning power pole and returned to the pool, not wanting to see the devastation of the outbuildings. He carried a bucket of water to the stands of gray Caucasians where all the hives were burning with a sweet smell of beeswax, and bees flew about in the little clouds above their old homes that were afire, honey, pollen, brood, all dying and burning. He wasted his bucket of water on them in bitter sorrow, and hopelessly went back to putting out a burning picket fence. In the distance he saw flames roaring on up over Mount Manuel. It had passed over the

ranch, the force of it here was finished, but it might burn a
week or a month up in the wilderness, depending on the intel-
ligence and honest efforts of firefighters.

After awhile the world spun and he couldn't see, and he
banged his head on a tree.

Greta found him blindly backed up against the scorched oak
in the yard.

"You okey dokey?"

"You?" he countered.

"I didn't get into it as much as you," she said. "You want me
to take you to the hospital?"

Tears leaked down his blackened face.

"Come here. I can't see," he said, not knowing whether his
eyes were open or not. "Please come here, Greta."

She touched him, took his burned hand, his arm, and put her
arm around his waist.

"Greta, I been a mixed up sonofabitch," he said.

"Sure. We just don't have much of a way of talking."

"You want to build it back?" He felt so tired he thought he'd
just hang his head down and sleep awhile.

"You betcha," she said, and then he wasn't hearing, just
dreaming a dream that was some kind of a race.

Sick and sore, he awakened next morning in the hospital.
Bandages covered his eyes and hands. The doctor assured him
that, in time, the burns would heal and he would see again,
and his hands would heal, and all he needed now was to rest
and rebuild.

In the darkness of his mind, he recalled the buildings going
up like firecrackers. All the fences burned. The waterline
burned, the water tank burned, bees, chickens, everything
burned except Billy who had stayed in the canyon until the
worst of of it had boiled over.

There was no way he could rebuild Apple Pie. The community was already too splintered by egocentric newcomers to
help and there was no insurance against a forest fire. Maybe if
he lived another thirty years, he could bring it back. But still,
how could he possibly rebuild chicken house and toolroom,

bees, fences, orchard, barn, woodshop, sheepshed? Why
bother? He felt weak, old, shaky, burned out.

Into his sightless lonely thoughts Greta asked, "How are
you doing, Harry?"

"I didn't hear you come in. Where are you staying?"

"At Apple Pie. The girls left. Moe is right here."

"But there's no water, no electricity, phone, nothing."

"We still got a roof, you know, and there's water in the
creek. Moe is a good waterboy."

"I try, Grampa," Moe patted his arm.

"I can't ever get the goddamned place shaped up, Gret. I'm
too old. Lost the ranch, and I'm done and beaten."

"Now watch your language," she said. "I want to give you
something to hold."

And suddenly as she guided a bundled baby into his ban-
daged hands, he couldn't believe what he knew.

"What?" he cried.

"Harry Junior," she said.

"Oh god, you're all really here," he said and sobbed.

Greta patted his shoulder and smoothed his wild white hair,
and Michael said, "I reckon you've got some help, Poppa," and
Sammy said, "Cheer up, Dad," and Gail said, "What do you
think of your little present?" and Jerry said, "All we needed
was a good excuse to come home."

He felt the tiny heart beating through the bandages, and
through his chest into his own heart, the little heart beating
inside his own.

Then again he clenched his jaw, waiting until he thought he
could speak like a man.

"Now you all," he said, "you be sure to look after your
Momma."